CRUSADE

More Warhammer 40,000 from Black Library

DARK IMPERIUM
Guy Haley

EISENHORN: XENOS
Dan Abnett

GAUNT'S GHOSTS:
THE FOUNDING OMNIBUS
Dan Abnett

CADIA STANDS
Justin D Hill

THE TALON OF HORUS
Aaron Dembski-Bowden

SIN OF DAMNATION
Gav Thorpe

ASSAULT ON BLACK REACH
Nick Kyme

THE DEVASTATION OF BAAL
Guy Haley

ASHES OF PROSPERO
Gav Thorpe

WAR OF SECRETS
Phil Kelly

CRUSADE

Andy Clark

BLACK LIBRARY

A BLACK LIBRARY PUBLICATION

First published in Great Britain in 2017 by
Black Library
This edition published in Great Britain in 2018 by
Black Library,
Games Workshop Ltd.,
Willow Road,
Nottingham, NG7 2WS, UK.

10 9 8 7 6 5 4 3 2 1

Produced by Games Workshop in Nottingham.
Cover illustration by Akim Kaliberda.

A CIP record for this book is available from the British Library.

ISBN 13: 978-1-78496-746-8

See Black Library on the internet at

blacklibrary.com

Find out more about Games Workshop
and the worlds of Warhammer 40,000 at

games-workshop.com

Printed and bound by CPI Group (UK) Ltd, Croydon, CR0 4YY

It is the 41st millennium. For more than a hundred centuries the Emperor has sat immobile on the Golden Throne of Earth. He is the Master of Mankind by the will of the gods, and master of a million worlds by the might of His inexhaustible armies. He is a rotting carcass writhing invisibly with power from the Dark Age of Technology. He is the Carrion Lord of the Imperium for whom a thousand souls are sacrificed every day, so that he may never truly die.

Yet even in his deathless state, the Emperor continues His eternal vigilance. Mighty battlefleets cross the daemon-infested miasma of the warp, the only route between distant stars, their way lit by the Astronomican, the psychic manifestation of the Emperor's will. Vast armies give battle in His name on uncounted worlds. Greatest amongst His soldiers are the Adeptus Astartes, the Space Marines, bioengineered super-warriors. Their comrades in arms are legion: the Astra Militarum and countless planetary defence forces, the ever-vigilant Inquisition and the tech-priests of the Adeptus Mechanicus to name only a few. But for all their multitudes, they are barely enough to hold off the ever-present threat from aliens, heretics, mutants – and worse.

To be a man in such times is to be one amongst untold billions. It is to live in the cruellest and most bloody regime imaginable. These are the tales of those times. Forget the power of technology and science, for so much has been forgotten, never to be re-learned. Forget the promise of progress and understanding, for in the grim dark future there is only war. There is no peace amongst the stars, only an eternity of carnage and slaughter, and the laughter of thirsting gods.

CHAPTER ONE

The augur probe Kalides-Gamma-19-8_6 floated in the void. It was an Imperial monitor satellite, a bulky mass of machinery and bio-reliquaric components slaved to a deep-space Mandeville point. Kalides-Gamma-19-8_6 had a single purpose: to monitor activity around the Kalides System's last stable warp translation point.

From here interstellar warships could break through from the strange dimension of the warp and begin their journey in-system. It fell to the augur probe, and several dozen more like it, to monitor all new arrivals and send word of their coming to the inhabited worlds deeper in-system.

Kalides-Gamma-19-8_6 had hung in place for decades. In that time, precisely twenty-seven starships had translated into real space beneath its watchful ocular receptors.

Now, came the twenty-eighth.

Auto-scriptoral data feeds scrolled through the probe's artificial cortex. Auto-inquisitions answered auspicatory sweep readings, but as its machine-spirit prepared to catalogue another uneventful sweep, the probe's cogitations were broken as a priority signum-interdiction signal flared within its empyric augurs.

The augur probe's void-hardened lenses refocused. Its empyric signums whirred to life, drinking in data on every spectrum as reality buckled. The starfield warped and rippled in a patch a hundred miles across. Light bent in the probe's staring fisheye-lens as though contorting in the grip of a black hole. Witchfires sparked and died in the darkness, each flare scorching the skin of reality.

Rents appeared, matter peeling away in strips like flesh from a leper's face, and ectoplasm spilled through, billowing in geysers and glowing with an eerie light.

Real space convulsed, crumpling and stretching all at once before ripping open like a fractal wound.

From within burst a starship.

It tumbled, engines firing as it fought to right itself. The ship's Geller field tattered amidst dancing corposants, revealing a craft almost a mile long, a buttressed Imperial warship whose battered hull plates were scorched and dented. Behind it, the tear in reality writhed madly, tendrils of dirty light groping blindly as if seeking to snatch back their prize before it could escape.

As the warp anomaly collapsed in upon itself and the starship sailed free, Kalides-Gamma-19-8_6 worked furiously to codify and categorise, to scan and transmit. Info-spools whirred within its armoured carapace, preparing a package of intelligence ready to be beamed through its aquila-carved macro-array. Machine-spirit interrogations determined the ship's designation as a strike cruiser – a Space Marine vessel. Further rapid auto-scans detected and classified the heraldry of the Ultramarines Chapter, from the noble world of Macragge.

The probe worked diligently, still attempting choristry with the on-board machine-spirits of the Ultramarines strike cruiser even as the warship bore down upon it. Retro-thrusters fired in the probe's flanks, trying to shunt it out of the starship's path, and Kalides-Gamma-19-8_6 was still busily compiling its vox-package when it was annihilated by the impact of the onrushing craft. The probe exploded, a brief starburst of fire against the armoured flank of the vessel.

It left a slight scorch mark upon the strike cruiser's starboard prow plating, directly below the ship's name: *Primarch's Sword*.

Within the armoured hull of the strike cruiser, a robed helot hastened along a corridor lit by strobing emergency lumens. He gripped the guide rails with one hand, ignoring the canted angle of the corridor and the shuddering gravity fluctuations. In his other hand, he clutched a freshly scribed data-parchment, intended for the eyes of the most important warriors on the ship.

He passed beneath the watchful eye-lenses of gothic gargoyles. He hurried across a gantry above a gun deck where servitors fought to extinguish fires and med-icae teams saw to the wounded. He brushed past other helots, each hurrying along on their own missions; many of his fellow servants were wounded, or hollow-eyed from lack of sleep.

The helot halted for a moment as the *Primarch's Sword* gave an especially violent jolt, and a groan of stressed metal rolled through the air. His eyes darted to the dark corners, whites shrinking around his pupils. He recalled the unnatural entities that had attempted to manifest during the strike cruiser's violent trip through warp space. The ship's Geller field had kept the warp-things at bay, but all the same the helot's thoughts turned to the reassuring weight of the bolt pistol holstered at his hip. No servant of the Ultramarines was defenceless…

'Emperor give your servant strength,' he muttered, 'and protect this unworthy soul from the terrors of the outer dark.'

Slowly the shuddering beneath his feet subsided, and the corridor righted itself as the *Primarch's Sword* restabilised its internal gravity. The helot made the sign of the aquila over the stylised white U emblazoned on his chest, then hurried on.

The helot arrived at the gold-embossed doors to the ship's strategium. Two Primaris Space Marines stood guard outside, bolt rifles held across their armoured chests. The warriors were demi-gods in the helot's eyes. Their fully enclosing suits of blue power armour, their proud helms with the faintly glowing eye-lenses, their thrumming back-mounted power packs – all of this filled him with a near-religious awe.

He approached with his eyes cast respectfully

downwards, and one of the Ultramarines nodded in acknowledgement.

'Proceed,' said the warrior, his vox-amplified voice a deep rumble.

The doors slid aside, and the helot passed into the strategium. The chamber was high-ceilinged and decorated with marble statuary. A huge hololithic table squatted at its centre, and banks of cogitators and strategic auspex shrines lined its walls. The strategium was large enough to hold twenty armoured Adeptus Astartes, but for now it contained just three Primaris Space Marines, the noble lords who led this strike force.

They were stood around the holotable, and their eyes turned to the helot as he entered. The gravity of their combined gaze almost pinned him in place.

He approached Lieutenant Cassian, holding out the data-parchment to the strike force's commanding officer.

'Missive from Shipmaster Aethor, my lord,' said the helot. 'He deemed it too urgent to await restoration of ship-wide vox.'

The Primaris lieutenant took the illuminated plastek printout, his noble features set in a stern frown.

'My thanks...'

'Kallem, my lord,' said the helot.

'My thanks, Kallem,' said Cassian. He unfurled the parchment, his eyes scanning its contents with inhuman speed.

'What is the word?' asked Librarian Keritraeus. The helot's eyes flicked involuntarily towards the psyker, drawn to the nest of cabling that punctured his scalp, and his dark eyes like wells of secrets.

'The shipmaster is pleased to inform us that, with the aid of Navigator X'gol, we have escaped the empyric storm that has gripped the ship these past days,' said Cassian.

'That much was obvious,' grunted Chaplain Dematris. The Chaplain's black armour and skull helm stood out in dark contrast to his comrades' blue armour. Dematris' mace-like crozius was laid on the holotable before him, a symbol of both his spiritual authority and his martial might.

'He goes on,' said Cassian dryly. 'The initial damage report from the tech-magi estimates the *Primarch's Sword* to be operating at fifty-two per cent combat effectiveness. We've lost several gun decks to fires and munitions detonations, and the aft void shield generators are inactive. Ship-wide vox is down, and we've lost more than half of the hull auspex.'

'And our warp drive?' asked Keritraeus.

'Magos Lamdaxh has been forced to render it quiescent for fear of empyric feedback or malefic overspill.'

'Then we are crippled,' said Dematris angrily. 'Without the power of our warp drive to pierce the veil, we are reduced to conventional drives. A journey that would take us days in warp space would require years under such conventional power. We have no way of rejoining the Indomitus Crusade, or even of letting our comrades know that we still live.'

'Does the honoured magos suggest how long it will take him to effect repairs?' asked Librarian Keritraeus.

'He does not,' replied Cassian. 'But let us assume for now that the gates of the warp are closed to us.'

'Then what is our course of action?' asked Dematris. 'We surely haven't succeeded in the pacification of Knossa only to be cast adrift in the interstellar darkness – that would not serve the Emperor's will.'

Lieutenant Cassian punched a runic sequence into the holotable, muttering the rites of awakening as he did so. The device flickered to life, crafting a three-dimensional map of local space in the air from light and shadow. The *Primarch's Sword* sat at its centre, a blue-and-gold rune, and around it the map slowly expanded as the ship's remaining auspicators wove a data-fresco of its surroundings.

'There are machine-spirit acknowledgements from deep-void satellites,' said Cassian. 'That would put us on the fringes of a star system, at least.'

'There,' said Keritraeus, pointing as further runes flickered into life. 'An asteroid belt. A gas giant. A death world.'

'More planets,' said Cassian, 'and with Imperial designators. By the Emperor's grace, we have come to a settled system, my brothers.'

Astrogation data scrolled down one side of the map. Names began to appear in flickering, High Gothic script as the bridge crew worked to triangulate their position.

'The Kalides System,' Cassian read aloud. 'And there, the capital world – Kalides Prime. Tithe-grade secundus, which would suggest sufficient orbital docks to hasten our repairs.'

'Even better...' said Keritraeus, tapping commands into the holotable's runic keys. The display focused on Kalides Prime, expanding the world into a slowly spinning orb and projecting additional information in a halo around it.

'An astropathic relay,' said Cassian, allowing himself a tight smile. 'This is good news. Not only can we repair the *Primarch's Sword*, but with the mind-choir of that planet's astropaths we can pierce the veil and send word to the Indomitus Crusade. We will let them know of our success on Knossa, and coordinate our rendezvous with the crusade fleet. We will return to the primarch's side.'

'Perhaps,' said Dematris. 'But let us take Knossa as a warning. According to this feed, the last confirmed contact with any world of the Kalides System was almost two years ago.'

'Not so unusual,' observed Keritraeus. 'The Imperium is a vast realm, and since the opening of the Great Rift it has been harder than ever to travel safely between the stars. This would hardly be the first isolated-yet-loyal system the Indomitus Crusade has brought back into the fold.'

'True,' said Dematris. 'But the corrupting influence of Chaos pervades the galaxy. Before the flesh-cults rose from the shadows to seize power, I don't doubt that Knossa was loyal also. Following the teachings of the primarch, I suggest the theoretical that we find ourselves in a hostile system until it is proven otherwise.'

'Wise counsel, Brother-Chaplain,' said Cassian. 'I will order Shipmaster Aethor to proceed under combat conditions, and have all battle-brothers stand ready for an engagement. Should the people of this system prove to be traitors, we will wrest control of Kalides Prime by force. We must be bellicose in this. Until we can achieve a true sidereal fix, it is impossible to know how much time we lost within the jaws of the warp. And we have our orders.'

Cassian keyed a sequence of runes, and the image of Kalides Prime was replaced by a towering warrior clad in magnificently ornamented armour. All but forgotten by the three Space Marines, Kallem gasped at the imposing sight of the Ultramarines' primarch, Roboute Guilliman. Even rendered in a grainy hololithic recording, the Lord of Ultramar exuded such a god-like presence that the helot was driven to his knees in awe.

'My sons,' said Guilliman, his voice rich, deep and utterly commanding. 'As the Indomitus Crusade gathers pace, we drive like a spear into the heartlands of my father's Imperium. So the dangers to our flanks grow manifold, and must be addressed. Captain Adrastean has already given you your orders, but allow me to say this to you. You are all newforged, all Primaris battle-brothers. You are the product of my will and Archmagos Cawl's labours. You are the ultimate warriors of the Imperium of Mankind, the torchbearers who will drive back the shadows in this darkest of hours. Know that you have my absolute faith. Let that knowledge strengthen your arms and gird your souls. Prevail, gloriously, swiftly, then return to my side. There are always more foes to be fought. The crusade must continue.'

The holorecording came to an end, and was replaced again by the image of Kalides Prime. Cassian, Keritraeus and Dematris looked at one another.

'We have a duty to perform, and no time to waste,'

said Cassian. 'We will not shame Captain Adrastean, and we will not fail our gene-sire.'

The lieutenant turned to face Kallem, who tried to control his shaking body and rose unsteadily to his feet.

'Kallem,' said Cassian. 'You will bear these orders to the shipmaster. He is to make all speed for Kalides Prime, and to stop for nothing. The magi and Techmarines are to make what repairs they can while en route. It will take us sixteen hours to reach the planet from this position, and I expect the *Primarch Sword*'s combat effectiveness to be increased at least twenty per cent by the time we do. External vox is to remain shrouded unless we receive Imperial hails first – the shipmaster should assume that we are in hostile space until it is proven otherwise.'

Kallem nodded, saluting the lieutenant with the sign of the aquila.

'At once, my lord.'

He turned and marched away, the image of the primarch's features still burned into his mind.

'Wise,' said Dematris as the doors slid shut behind the helot. 'Replaying that holorecording. It stoked the fires of that man's faith, and those flames will spread.'

Cassian smiled. 'It was for our benefit as much as his, Dematris.'

'Sixteen hours, then,' said Keritraeus. 'Ample time to prepare ourselves for whatever lies ahead. I will meditate, and focus my powers. Passage through the warp storm was… unpleasant. I need to refortify my mind.'

'I will look to matters spiritual,' said Dematris, hefting his crozius. 'There will be those who wish to make their devotions in the Reclusiam. Besides which, duty requires reconsecration.'

'It will be good to wield that blade again,' said Cassian. 'Almost enough to make me hope that Kalides *does* play host to heretics.'

'Always hope for enemies to slay,' quoted Dematris. 'For in their spilled blood will the Imperium be washed clean.'

Keritraeus raised one eyebrow, but made no comment.

'Very good, brothers,' said Cassian. 'Muster will commence when we are six hours out.'

'Until then,' said Keritraeus.

The Librarian and the Chaplain departed, leaving Lieutenant Cassian standing alone before the slowly revolving image of Kalides Prime. He stared hard at the hololith, as though he could force it to give up its secrets. There was much to be done, he thought. Strategic inloads of the planet's topography, settlement maps, last-known military strengths and the like. Then construction of likely battlefield theoreticals and the practical solutions to them, as the primarch taught. A tour of the ship for the sake of morale, and then his own personal preparations: the rites of arming over his wargear, and meditations to centre himself.

'But first,' he murmured, 'to stoke those fires of faith.'

The ship-wide vox might still be crippled, but Space Marine armour was a marvel of arcane technology. Alongside the suites of auto-senses that sharpened their battlefield perceptions, and the servo-bundles that augmented their already prodigious strength, every Primaris battle-brother's Mark X armour incorporated a hardened vox-emitter keyed to a set of coded command channels. This vox-net was impervious to all but the most devastating forms of disruption, and so as Cassian keyed his vox-bead to channel ultima, he knew that his address would reach every one of the seventy-two other Ultramarines aboard the *Primarch's Sword*.

'My brothers,' began Cassian. Throughout the vessel, Primaris Space Marines ceased what they were doing and attended to their lieutenant's words.

'My brothers, on Knossa we crushed the heretic foe,' he said. 'We threw down the twisted idols of Chaos and we purged the degenerates that had fallen to their worship. We brought the light of the Indomitus Crusade to those benighted by heresy. We won victory in the primarch's name.'

Upon the ship's firing ranges, Intercessor battle-brothers held up their bolt rifles in salute, while heavily armoured Aggressors clenched their power fists and raised them triumphantly.

'Upon our departure from that system, the foul powers of the empyrean attempted to punish us for our victory,' continued Cassian. 'Yet even the fury of a warp storm could not hold us back from our duty. We escaped. We endured.'

Knelt in meditation in the ship's Reclusiam, the brothers of Sergeant Marcus' Reiver squad let the lieutenant's words echo through their minds, even as they prepared to don their sinister wargear and the terrifying personas that went with it.

'Now, the Emperor has provided us with the means

to contact the crusade forces again, and to repair our craft that we might rejoin our battle-brothers all the sooner. But the greatest gifts are not given freely. The Emperor's beneficence must be earned, and there is every chance that we will find a world turned to madness and heresy by the malign influence of the Great Rift.'

Upon the arming deck, the brothers of Sergeant Gallen's Hellblaster squad looked up from their prayers over the bellicose machine-spirits of their plasma incinerators. They shared stern, stoic glances, the looks of warriors committed to giving everything – even their lives – if victory demanded it.

'Perhaps we will find a world of faithful Imperial servants, ready to aid our cause,' said Cassian. 'But if not, then know this – we will crush anyone foolish enough to oppose us. We will lay low any heretic who dares stand between us and our return to the primarch's side. We are the gene-sons of Roboute Guilliman, and we will prevail. For the Emperor!'

'For the Emperor!' cried Cassian's warriors, their booming voices carrying along the ship's corridors and through its cavernous chambers, filling their helot servants with pride and courage.

'Muster begins at seventeen hundred hours shiptime,' said Cassian. 'Look to your wargear and ready yourselves for battle. If enemies await us, we shall make them rue their folly...'

CHAPTER TWO

'Generosity,' said Lord Gurloch. The Lord of Contagion's voice was deep and wet, bubbling with the rancid sweat that seeped through his body both inside and out. 'Generosity is the watchword of Grandfather Nurgle. It is the first rule of our god, and we who worship him must follow his divine example. It is how we show our faith.'

Gurloch stood amidst the mould-furred rubble of the Mons Aquilas counting house, addressing his followers. He wore fluid-streaked Terminator plate, his bloated flesh spilling through corroded rents, and though the warriors he addressed were hulking Plague Marines, he loomed over them all.

'Take our enemies,' Gurloch said, stomping forwards. His brothers parted to let him through, their armour joints seeping and respirators gurgling. 'They show no generosity of spirit. No magnanimity, and though we bring them plentiful gifts, they offer nothing in return. And thus, they suffer.'

Gurloch halted at the edge of the ruins and stared up the processional roadway, to where the astropathic fortress stood beneath skies clotted with sluggish clouds. The structure was vast and imposing, yet it cowered behind its flickering banks of void shields. It stood silent and alone amidst the war-torn remains of Kalides Prime's capital city, a vast and now ruined sprawl named Dustrious.

'I hate them, of course,' said Gurloch. 'For their ignorance, their worship of the Corpse-Emperor. For their blinkered refusal to accept the true might of the Dark Gods, and the glory of Nurgle above all. But I pity them, also.'

'What is there… to pity… my lord?' asked Thrax, Gurloch's favoured lieutenant. Thrax was a Biologis Putrifier, a plague alchemist whose armour was festooned with clinking alembics and experimental blight grenades. His voice escaped his helm's respirator like that of a drowning man, snatches of words gasped through the fluids that bubbled in his lungs.

'Thrax, these wretches have been deprived,' said Gurloch with an expansive gesture. 'They refuse to share the psychic bounty of their astropaths only because their God-Emperor has taught them to be grasping, cruel and selfish. He has taught them that only through suffering can their lives have meaning, that freedom and empowerment are just clever names for damnation. I pity them that their faith is built upon weakness, upon clinging to what little they have and refusing to give or receive the gifts that could be theirs. We must set an example, and show them a better way.'

As he spoke, the boom of artillery fire rolled through the air. Gurloch raised his horned helm and watched as shells sailed up from behind the counting house and arced down to burst against the fortress' shields. Dirty flame blossomed and the void shields flickered, their efforts becoming more frenetic as thick clouds of black spores spilled from the blasts and whirled across their glowing surface.

'We still cannot… breach their shields… at range… my lord,' said Thrax. 'And… Imperial forces survive… in the Temple District. They continue to… harass our flanks. If Plaguelord Morbidius… returns before we secure this… sanctum… then he will… punish us for our failure.'

'Patience, Thrax,' replied Gurloch in a tone of genuine good cheer. 'Battle should be steady, drawn out, savoured to the last dribbles of blood and pus. Entropy is our ally. Suffering is our gift. Starvation, despair, the inevitability of disease – these are the vectors by which our god's power spreads. So Mortarion teaches us.'

'Dark praises upon… the primarch,' gurgled Thrax.

'Dark praises upon the primarch,' echoed Gurloch before continuing. 'Eventually, our enemies will concede defeat, Thrax. And as for the Imperial Guardsmen lurking in the Temple District, let them try to fight us! Let them pit their paltry strength against the indomitable might of the Death Guard! I applaud their tenacity, and relish the utter hopelessness of their cause. Let us give them suffering and sickness that they might, in their turn, aid our true purpose here. Let us be… *generous.*'

ANDY CLARK

Gurloch turned to the assembled Plague Marines, hefting his massive plaguereaper axe high.

'We are the sons of Mortarion!' he roared, clotted matter spraying from his vox-grille. 'We are the warriors of the Third Plague Company of Mortarion's Anvil, blessed with the Everseep, the Endless Suppuration, the Weeping Gift of Nurgle himself!'

His brothers waved bolters, blades, heavy maces and rot-nozzled plague spewers. Their cheer was ghastly, a gurgling drone that sounded like a herd of grox drowning in swamp water.

'We are entropy personified!' cried Gurloch. 'We are the death inevitable, the inexorable wasting, and we will grind these heathens down until they give us what we want.'

His warriors gave another mighty cry, almost drowning out the roar of their Plagueburst Crawlers lobbing another volley of shells towards the fortress.

'Ready your weapons, and bring up another batch of cages,' ordered Gurloch. 'Let us offer them our gifts again.'

Throughout the ruins, the warriors of Gurloch's vectorium trudged into position with their bolters ready. They would advance into range of the fortress' shields and then lay down harassing fire, continuing to probe the enemy defences. They likely had the numbers and the fortitude to carry the day if they wished, but by Gurloch's order, they would not push up the slopes to the fortress walls themselves.

Not yet.

That duty would fall instead to other, lesser beings. He saw them now, packed tightly into huge, rusting cages that ground through the ruins on industrial tracks. The creatures' eyes stared mindlessly into the middle distance. Their rictus grins dripped with slime. Their rotting flesh and squirming tentacles stank of putrefaction, and their moans filled the air.

'My poxwalkers,' said Gurloch, his tone that of a proud parent.

The tracked cages lurched to a halt, well out of range of the fortress' guns. Locking bolts blew and the cage doors swung open with shuddering clangs. Groaning sorrowfully through their rotten smiles, the diseased former populace of Dustrious stumbled from their cages and shambled towards the fortress. Some clutched crude clubs and rusting tools. Others brandished firearms, though Gurloch knew that none of them had the wit to use them.

They were not the first such attack wave unleashed upon the astropathic fortress. Many thousands of their fellows already formed gory mounds around its walls. The combined stench of their gas-bloated corpses was ghastly, and Gurloch breathed a deep draught as he watched his latest attack wave advance.

Thousands of the mindless never-dead swarmed through the ruins and began the stumbling ascent towards the Imperial fortress. Gurloch's brothers strode behind them like shepherds, while from the rear lines the Plagueburst Crawlers maintained their steady bombardment.

The guns of the astropathic fortress came to life. Heavy bolters and autocannons roared, mowing down rank upon rank of plague-ridden mutants. Battle cannons hammered shells into their midst, raising geysers of foul fluids and spinning limbs, but the poxwalkers advanced undaunted, as incapable of fear as they were of escaping their own dreadful fate.

'Shall we… join the attack… my lord?' asked Thrax, caressing the brittle glass alembics that hung from his armour. 'I have concoctions… I wish to perfect.'

'Small chance at such a range,' said Gurloch. 'No, let the poxwalkers soak up our enemy's fire and gnaw away at their munitions. Let them groan their fulsome dirge, that it might seep into the minds of unwary defenders and sow the seeds of sickness in their dreams. I have need of your concoctions elsewhere, Thrax.'

'The… Imperial Guard?' asked Thrax.

'Perhaps,' said Gurloch, 'but perhaps not. Blorthos has had a vision – something he believes worthy of my attention. Let us take his Witherlings and see for ourselves.'

Gurloch turned away from the ongoing slaughter and stomped through the ruins, Thrax lumbering at his side.

A half hour later, Gurloch led Thrax and the Witherlings down a deep drainage trench between rows of gargoyle-encrusted hab-blocks. He waded hip-deep through rancid sewage, clouds of fat flies droning around him.

The Witherlings were almost as massive as their master, a band of five Blightlord Terminators whose hulking armour drizzled unclean fluids and crawled with corrosion. They were led by their grotesque champion, Blorthos, whose helm was little more than a rusted frame for a bulbous eye the size of a man's head. The dripping orb was milky with cataracts and threaded through with burrowing worms, yet still it rolled back and forth in its setting, following movements only he could see.

'Up ahead, my lord,' rumbled the Terminator. 'There is a tunnel, and beyond it–'

'The munitions manufactorum,' said Gurloch. 'Yes, this is its primary run-off channel, is it not? Then your vision concerned Slaugh and his squad?'

'The Grandfather gifts me fever dreams, my lord,' replied Blorthos. 'They are vivid, but rarely lucid. I saw this place, and a threat to our brothers – sharp needles digging through rotten flesh, but little more.'

'Of course, of course,' said Gurloch. 'It is not for such as us to question the glorious gifts of the Grandfather.'

'What was… Slaugh… doing in this region?' asked Thrax. 'There have… been no reports of… Imperial activity here for… several weeks now. Not since… our initial… drop.'

'No indeed,' replied Gurloch. 'A hearty bombardment of slitherpox and churning lung put paid to any who took refuge, and the Imperials have not dared to set foot here since, lest they feel the touch of Nurgle upon their flesh. No, Thrax, this was not intended to be a combat mission. I merely sent Slaugh to hunt out any munitions stockpiles that we could turn to our use should our constant generosity lead our own guns to feel the pinch of famine.'

'Seems Slaugh may have felt the pinch of something else,' chuckled Blorthos. There was no love lost between Gurloch's champions, who were forever locked in competition.

'We shall see soon enough,' said Gurloch, as he waded on into the shadow of the cavernous inflow pipe. The flanks of the manufactorum reared overhead, and for a moment it felt to Gurloch as though he were advancing into the maw of some immense beast. He grinned at the thought – anything foolish enough to devour him would soon find itself poisoned beyond words – and led the way into the darkness.

'Here is… another one,' called Thrax. Gurloch looked up from the sprawled body of Slaugh and grunted in irritation.

'All of them, then,' he said.

He and his followers stood amidst the massive labour-belts and rusting machinery of the manufactorum. The work-floor was carpeted with the contorted remains of the hundreds of labour serfs who had died here weeks earlier. Amongst them, Gurloch had found the corpses of Slaugh's squad. Their armoured forms had not been difficult to locate.

'They died without firing a shot,' said Blorthos contemptuously. 'They sent no message.' His Terminators stood in a rough ring around their leaders, facing outwards with their guns raised.

'It must… have been swift,' said Thrax, glancing at the deep shadows wreathing the manufactorum. 'An ambush…'

Gurloch switched through his helm's visual filters, each one a noxious shade of rust, rot or poison, and began cogitating ballistic trajectories and assessing impact points.

'Accurate,' he mused. 'And deadly. These shots hit

eyes, armour joints, corroded plates. They punched right through the blessed flesh of our brothers and killed them as though they were flimsy loyalists.'

'The Astra Militarum must have sent snipers,' said Blorthos, but he sounded doubtful.

'Our enemies have neither the marksmanship nor the weapons to achieve this,' replied Gurloch. 'No, brothers, Grandfather Nurgle has blessed us with a warning. Some other power is at work here, and we must be wary. Thrax – vox Phlegorius, if you would. Let us have our plague surgeon cut these corpses up and inspect the rounds that killed them. Besides, he will need to reclaim their gene-seed for the Legion before it becomes too flyblown to be of use. I–'

Gurloch was interrupted by the dull tolling of his helm vox. He activated it, and heard the voice of Ruptus, one of his Plague Marine champions.

'My lords, the assault upon the astropathic sanctum has reached the third firing line,' gargled Ruptus, *'but the Astra Militarum have launched another attack. They are pushing tanks and infantry out of the Temple District into sectors six and seven.'*

'They timed their strike well,' said Gurloch. 'We are extended on the attack, and I am at a remove from the battle.'

'Perhaps… this was their… work… after all?' asked Thrax. 'A… ruse to… pull you away?'

'The Imperials could not have sent me my vision,' snorted Blorthos.

'No,' said Gurloch. 'Yet still the timing is fortuitous, is it not? Ah well, the heavier the rain, the swifter the crops rot, and we cannot win Nurgle's blessings without opportunities to excel. Ruptus, spread the word – all vectorium forces are to pull back and reinforce against the Imperial Guard. Leave the poxwalkers to press their attack. They will not last much longer anyway.'

'*Yes, my lord,*' said Ruptus over the vox.

'You shall oversee the defence until I return, Ruptus,' continued Gurloch. 'Give ground slowly – concentrate on exhausting their forces and eliminating their armour wherever possible. And send Pustulus' and Thrombox's squads to sector nine. Have them bring a couple of bloat-drones, hmm? We will congeal with his forces on our way back and hit the Imperial flank, severing the spear tip of their advance.'

'*In Mortarion's name, my lord,*' said Ruptus, cutting the vox-link.

'It seems Phlegorius has been saved a walk,' said Gurloch.

'Lord?' asked Thrax.

'Whether or not our enemies staged this diversion, they have made best use of it,' said Gurloch, staring out into the gloom. 'And we must assume that the assassins that killed Slaugh and his brothers are still at large. No, I will not risk our best plague surgeon at this juncture. Blorthos, you and your brothers heft a corpse each. We will bring them with us, that Phlegorius may examine them at his leisure.'

Gurloch saw Blorthos stiffen; he knew that the Terminator would resent this demeaning duty. He also knew that no warrior of the Death Guard would complain at such a hardship, lest their fortitude be questioned.

'Yes, lord,' said Blorthos, motioning to his brothers

to choose and heft a corpse each. Blorthos himself threw Slaugh's body over one shoulder as though his armoured remains weighed nothing at all.

'Good,' said Gurloch. 'Let us away. Battle calls.'

Captain Dzansk, commander of the Cadian 44th Heavy Infantry, cursed as something struck the flank of his Chimera. The armoured personnel carrier rocked on its suspension, throwing Dzansk and his command squad around in their restraints.

'What in Throne's name was that?' barked Colour Sergeant Weims as the vehicle skidded to a halt.

'No clue,' said Dzansk. 'Nothing good.'

He banged a fist on the hatch to the drivers' compartment, ignoring the ache in his bones from whatever heretical ague he had contracted.

'Hey, Stranson, what–'

Dzansk was cut off as their transport bucked again, lurching backwards with a shriek of tortured metal. Dzansk heard muffled screams from the drivers' compartment, followed by a loud bang. Smoke began to leak through the ventilation ports.

'Damnit,' said Dzansk. 'Chonsky, get the hatch. Weapons ready – we're disembarking.'

Gunner Chonsky hefted his meltagun with one hand and hit the hatch-release rune with the other. The Chimera's rear ramp opened with a hydraulic whine, allowing thick smoke and buzzing flies to spill inside.

Chonsky was first down the ramp, coughing on the foul air that had already poisoned their lungs thrice over. Dzansk followed, but pulled up with a yell of alarm as huge metal tentacles whipped out of the fug and punched through Chonsky's chest. The gunner screamed as he was hefted off the ground, his wild eyes locking with Dzansk's in the split second before the rusted tendrils ripped him bloodily in two.

Looming through miasmal smoke and spores came a Helbrute Dreadnought, a hulking giant of rusted metal and rotten flesh taller than Dzansk's burning Chimera. One arm comprised the waving tentacles that had ripped Chonsky apart, while the other mounted a massive cannon. A cluster of eyes rolled above a fleshy maw in the thing's chest, which was itself an armoured sarcophagus housing the tortured flesh remnant of the machine's pilot, a once-great Death Guard champion.

'Down!' shouted Dzansk, diving aside as the iron-clad monster opened fire. Shells whipped over him in a storm, reducing Medicae Danvers and Colour Sergeant Weims to bloody gobbets.

Voxman Kavier hit the ground next to Dzansk, swearing inaudibly over the din of the fusillade. The Helbrute's fire tore through the open hatch of the Chimera and detonated its engines. The explosion was shockingly enormous. It picked up Dzansk and hurled him past the Helbrute, leaving his ears ringing and his body bruised as he rolled to a stop.

Dzansk looked up groggily through the swirling smoke and saw the Dreadnought turning towards him. Its fanged maw yawned and its eyes rolled madly. There were more shapes in the murk: Cadian Guardsmen and tanks firing as they advanced, but none were close enough to come to his aid.

Dzansk rolled sideways, frantically avoiding the lash of the Helbrute's tentacles. He ripped his laspistol from its holster and fired, bursting one of the creature's eyes with a lucky shot. It roared, though the sound was still muffled to Dzansk, and stomped towards him.

He saw Kavier, lying on his side, unmoving – no help there. He prayed to the Emperor for aid, scrambling to his feet and swatting away droning flies. His eyes alighted on Chonsky's meltagun, lying discarded near the bloodied remains of its former owner. He dived for the gun, feeling everything inside him constrict in terror as the Helbrute's tentacles whipped past mere inches from his flesh.

Captain Dzansk hit the ground in a roll and came up with Chonsky's meltagun levelled.

'Oh spirit of the weapon, forgive my crude ministrations and vent thine wrath upon this unclean thing,' he prayed, then squeezed the trigger.

The meltagun's energy blast built from a hiss to a roar in a split second. The Helbrute reeled as a column of super-agitated microwave energy bored through its sarcophagus and struck the clotted remnants of the Death Guard warrior interred within. Boiling flesh and warp flame jetted from the glowing hole, and the machine gave a ululating howl as it staggered backwards. Something exploded within its armoured frame, smoke belched and the war engine toppled, crashing down mere feet from Dzansk.

'Emperor be praised,' whispered the Cadian captain. He shook himself out of his daze and rushed over to Voxman Kavier. To his relief, his comrade was stirring and groaning – wounded, ill, but very much alive.

Dzansk grabbed the headset attached to his vox-man's backpack and dialled into the Cadian command channel, listening as he scrolled hastily through strategic data on his auspex.

'–eventh Platoon retreating, repeat, Seventh Platoon retreating, overwhelming enemy fire at–'

'–what in Throne's name is that thing? Watch out, don't–'

'–questing immediate fire on these coordinates, one-four-one-two, repea–'

'–coming from the flank. Holy Cadia, are those Terminators? We have to–'

'Men and women of Cadia!' barked Dzansk, overriding their vox-channels so all would hear. 'I am sounding the retreat. Enemy flanking forces are attempting to bifurcate our advance and trap our forward elements between their guns. Fourth, Eighth and Twelfth Platoons – fall back immediately to position Thades and filter out through the ruins. Lieutenant Bronski, get your squadron out of there and punch out to the right flank, *Vengeance* to the fore. We need your battle tanks intact. Everyone else, fall back by squads, cover pattern Alphaus, and rendezvous at the Shrine of the Emperor's Beatific Countenance. Cadia stands!'

Confirmations flooded back through the vox, and Dzansk felt a moment of pride at how efficiently his warriors fought, even in conditions as terrible as these. The thunder of Death Guard bolters echoed through the murk, spurring the captain to action. He hoisted Kavier onto his feet, ignoring the voxman's pained groans and the blood that caked his scalp. Throwing one of Kavier's arms over his shoulder and clutching Chonsky's meltagun tight, Dzansk began a hurried limp back towards the Imperial lines. He heard the ragged wheeze in his breathing, and ignored it.

'Emperor,' he prayed as he hobbled through the murk. 'If you're listening, I know we're no more deserving than anyone else, and I'm sure you've got better things to do than listen to my pathetic bloody prayers, but if you can hear me, please, send us your aid. I don't think we're going to last much longer without it.'

CHAPTER THREE

The embarkation deck of the *Primarch's Sword* resounded with activity. Squads of Primaris Space Marines jogged into position in preparation to board heavily armoured gunships. Munitions servitors lumbered between the strike force's vehicles, hefting shells and power packs into place with their servo-arms, or hauling sloshing fuel bowsers.

Helots hurried back and forth, bearing equipment, orders and artefacts for their masters. Chaplain Dematris marched along the lines of warriors, leading them in chanting the Chapter's rites of battle, while cyber-cherubim fluttered through the strobing light, carrying censers which trailed thick incense smoke. All the bustle and activity was framed against the star-speckled darkness of space, visible through the deck's open blast doors but held at bay by a shimmering force field.

Lieutenant Cassian and Librarian Keritraeus stood on an observation gantry, watching the final preparations.

'It appears you will get your war, lieutenant,' said the Librarian.

'You make me sound like some bellicose Space Wolf or Black Templar,' said Cassian. 'I am not champing at the bit for bloodshed, Keritraeus. But I won't shy from doing the Emperor's work, or from admitting it brings me satisfaction.'

'Nor should you, Cassian,' said the Librarian with a faint smile. 'But have a caution. I know that Captain Adrastean placed a substantial burden of responsibility upon your shoulders. Be sure you don't allow it to force your hand.'

'I don't deny I have much to prove,' said Cassian. 'To Adrastean. To the primarch.'

'To yourself?' asked Keritraeus.

Cassian nodded. 'That too. This war has raged for ten thousand years, my friend, and we are latecomers. We have not shared the burdens, nor endured the hardships, that others have. There are those, even amongst the armies of the Indomitus Crusade, who still doubt us for what we are.'

Keritraeus chuckled softly.

'My brother, look at whom you are speaking to,' he said. 'Since the earliest days of the Imperium, there have been voices raised against my kind. Witches, they call us, unnatural and dangerous. That has never stopped the Librarians of the Space Marine Chapters from using our powers to aid our battle-brothers, shield the Emperor's servants and slaughter His enemies.'

'A wise comparison, brother,' replied Cassian. 'One I hope we can live up to.'

'We shall soon see. It appears that Dematris has concluded his prayers.'

'Good. Then in Guilliman's name, let us be about it.'

Cassian stepped up to the railing and keyed his vox-grille to amplify his voice.

'Brothers,' he said, voice booming through the embarkation deck. 'Once again, we prepare to do battle with the dark forces of Chaos.'

His warriors cheered.

'Within minutes, the *Primarch's Sword* will enter high orbit above Kalides Primes. Though atmospheric conditions are poor, from long-range auspex and oracular interrogation we can surmise that the planet has been invaded by the Heretic Astartes. Brothers, we face the Death Guard.'

A murmur ran through the ranks at this. The Death Guard were one of the original Traitor Legions – ancient warriors, steeped in corruption and seething with the power of Chaos.

This would be a hard fight.

'We have detected the wreckage of several Imperial Navy warships scattered through the planet's upper atmosphere,' continued Cassian. 'We have also marked warp translation signatures that suggest where our enemy's craft came and went, leaving us with orbital supremacy. Moreover, the capital city's astropathic fortress remains intact, and there are at least some Imperial ground forces still engaging the invaders. Do not make the mistake of believing that any of this will make our mission easier. The Death Guard seem to be warding themselves from our auguries in some fashion. Strategic intelligence is thus fragmentary, but hints at enemy numbers substantially greater than our own. Also, the foe has control of the capital city's orbital defence batteries.

'You have all been briefed upon the plan. We will execute a combat drop to capture the orbital batteries while Shipmaster Aethor uses starship wreckage to shield the *Primarch's Sword* from any return fire. Once the batteries are ours, we will bring the strike cruiser lower to provide supporting bombardments, link up with any localised Imperial forces and drive for the astropathic fortress. We will do this swiftly, before the enemy can marshal their strength, and we will do it in the name of the Emperor and the primarch!'

'For the Emperor!' roared his warriors. 'For Guilliman!'

Inceptor Sergeant Polandrus depressed a runic stud in his gauntlet, causing a ceramite heat shield to slide down over his helm. He flexed his limbs, feeling the motor-bundles of his Mark X Gravis power armour respond smoothly, before depressing his heels and causing his servo-stirrups to give, then resist. He interrogated his weapon-feeds, ensuring they were clear of obstruction and their ammunition counts were at maximum.

'Final checks, brothers,' he voxed, casting an eye over his two comrades as they underwent their own pre-drop rituals. The Inceptors looked unwieldy in their heat-shielded armour, with their heavy jump packs and their guns underslung on their forearms. Polandrus knew better.

His battle-brothers confirmed their readiness, and Polandrus nodded in satisfaction, activating his helm's drop protocols and watching as wireframe flight vectors overlaid themselves on his vision. He glanced across at Inceptor Squad Thaddean, their comrades in arms for over a decade now, readying themselves nearby.

'Ready, brother?' asked Polandrus over the vox.

'To slaughter heretics?' asked Sergeant Thaddean. 'Always.'

'For the glory of Ultramar, then,' said Polandrus. 'Inceptor Squads Polandrus and Thaddean commencing atmospheric insertion drop in three, two, one…'

Feeding power through his armour's systems, Polandrus began a pounding run across the embarkation deck. His brothers followed, their steps becoming bounding springs as servo-stirrups took their weight and propelled them forwards. The Inceptors engaged their jump packs, blue firelight flaring within their jet nozzles, and led by Polandrus they accelerated towards the lip of the embarkation deck, the void of space and the immensity of Kalides Prime yawning dizzyingly below.

The brink came up to meet Polandrus and he leapt, propelling himself through the deck's force field and into the cold emptiness of space.

In a moment, the din of gunship engines and autoloaders was gone, replaced by the sound of his steady breathing, the dull thump of his twin hearts and the clipped vocalisations of the squad vox. He fed power to his thrusters and tucked his limbs in at his sides as he angled himself towards Kalides Prime and began his descent.

'Squad, report,' he said. His battle-brothers voxed in, confirming that they had successfully exited the *Primarch's Sword* and were following him in towards the thermosphere.

'Sergeant Thaddean?' asked Polandrus.

'We're away,' came Thaddean's voice. *'Smooth deployment. Coordinates locked in. We will follow you down.'*

'On wings of fire, brother,' said Polandrus. With a few quick bursts of thrust, he turned his arcing flight into a level descent, watching the runes designating his squadmates as they all settled into their drop vectors. Beneath him, Kalides grew larger by the second while the starfield slowly dimmed. At his back, the *Primarch's Sword* descended more slowly, gunships beginning to boost out of its launch bays as it came.

The gunships would be the second wave; the Inceptors had the honour of being the first.

'Entering upper atmosphere in five,' voxed Thaddean. *'Brace.'*

Polandrus felt his armour's servos stiffen and his posture lock as its machine-spirit baffled him against the impending gravitic forces. He muttered a prayer for the Emperor to watch over him, then flames were licking across his armour's plates as he began re-entry. Thermosensors registered steep spikes, and a bone-deep shuddering ran through his body, fierce enough that a lesser being would quickly have been rendered unconscious.

'Watch your angles,' he voxed. 'Brother Ulandro, adjust point two – you're a little steep.'

Flames were blazing around him now as he punched

down through Kalides' atmospheric envelope. Thermic warnings continued to ping. He felt his momentum and weight increase as the planet's gravity reached up to take him in its embrace, and a constant roar filled his senses.

Polandrus felt no fear. This was what he was made for.

The fires died in an instant, replaced by the vertiginous sensation of full gravity and the churning mass of the planet's polluted storm clouds rushing up to meet him.

'Reading high winds within the storm system,' he voxed.

'*Acknowledged,*' replied Thaddean. '*Detecting trace malefic energies within the clouds.*'

'Confirmed,' said Polandrus. 'Intone the litany of denial, brothers. Gird your souls.'

The Inceptors streaked down like missiles, maintaining a grim chant as they punched into the cloud layer. Polandrus gritted his teeth as visibility dropped to virtually nil and furious cross-winds pummelled him. Greasy rain streaked the lenses of his helm, and as green-tinged lightning flashed around him, he thought he saw the suggestion of leering visages swirling hugely amidst the thunderheads.

'Keep your coordinates locked, brothers,' he ordered. 'Trust in the machine-spirits of your armour. Follow drop vectors and be ready for combat landing in one hundred and eighty seconds.'

Lightning flared in strobing blasts. The clouds formed fanged maws the size of hab-blocks that yawned wide and closed over them. Thunder crashed and the winds howled, while storm rain hammered the Inceptors' armour with the force of shotgun pellets.

Through it all they held their course, and as his helm altimeter spiralled downwards, Polandrus unlocked his drop posture and roused the wrathful machine-spirits of his assault bolters.

'Breaking cloud cover in three, two...' Polandrus shot through the last wisps of cloud, and the ruined city-scape of Dustrious was revealed below him.

'The city is in an advanced state of deterioration,' he voxed, opening his channel to the entire strike force. 'Visual confirmation – large portions of Dustri-ous have been bombarded from orbit. Damage and auspex readings suggest a mixture of conventional munitions and malefic contaminants. Malefic con-tagion levels high throughout the city. Confirming status of astropathic fortress... It appears intact and shielded at this time.'

'Orbital batteries sighted on southern edge of the city, coordinates one-one-seven-three-one,' added Thaddean. *'Auspex reads enemy presence confirmed on site.'*

'Commencing final approach,' said Polandrus. 'Emperor guide our aim.'

With a thought, Polandrus increased the thrust from his jump pack, accelerating into an almost suicidal dive. As he did so, lights flashed amongst the batteries below, muzzle flare sparking amongst metal gantries and illuminating the flanks of huge las silos.

'They've spotted us,' said Thaddean.

'It won't save them,' said Polandrus.

Shots whipped around him. Flak shells burst in clouds of dirty smoke, shrapnel sparking off his armour plates. Warning chimes sounded as threat recognition runes blossomed across his field of vision.

'Landing zone confirmed,' he said, jinking to evade a sawing line of flak fire. 'Roof of generatorum seven-alpha. Light enemy presence. Deploy on my mark.'

Polandrus and his warriors streaked downwards at punishing speed, using their sheer momentum to confound their enemy's aim. The generatorum swelled before them, a blocky building nestled amidst the looming barrels of the las silos, its flanks thick with industrial piping and its roof a flat expanse dotted with huge cooling vents.

Enemy warriors were visible between them, ragged human cultists who pointed and screamed as they sprayed autogun fire skywards.

Polandrus waited until collision alarms were shrilling in his helm, then triggered his landing thrusters. Retrorockets fired with body-blow force, spinning him in the air so that his feet were pointed groundwards. His heavy jump pack howled as it arrested his descent, and he hit the generatorum roof with enough force to crack the ferrocrete, his servo-stirrups absorbing the shock that would otherwise have broken every bone in his legs.

Polandrus swung his assault bolters up, ballistic cogitations and targeter runes dropping into place over his vision. He depressed his firing runes and sent a hail of mass-reactive bolts thumping into the cultists on the rooftop. The bolt shells leapt away on blazing propellant trails, and as each one punched through flak armour and flesh, the micro-cogitators built into their warheads detected sufficient surrounding mass to trigger detonation. Four luckless worshippers of Nurgle exploded in as many seconds, the diseased blessings of their god powerless to save them.

'For the Emperor!' roared Polandrus.

His brothers slammed down beside him, their fire joining his own. A hurricane of bolt shells whipped outwards, the Inceptors' firing solutions perfectly cogitated to prevent them from catching each other in their overlapping fields of fire.

Cultists burst one after another, blood spraying across the rooftop, severed limbs spinning away. Skulls detonated. Bone shrapnel flew. In under twenty seconds, Polandrus and his two battle-brothers killed all thirty of the Chaos cultists occupying the rooftop. Their enemy's ragged fire barely scratched their armour.

'Squad Polandrus, drop insertion successful,' voxed the sergeant.

'*Squad Thaddean, drop insertion successful,*' echoed his comrade. Polandrus glanced over at a shuttle pad some hundred yards to the east. Thaddean's squad had landed there, and had slaughtered their enemies with little resistance.

'*Well done, brothers,*' voxed Lieutenant Cassian. '*Drop craft on approach. Commence stage two.*'

'Confirmed,' replied Polandrus.

A spread of runic designators lit up on his auspex, each one indicating a flak battery that could pose a risk to the Ultramarines gunships even now streaking down through the cloud cover overhead.

'*Good hunting,*' voxed Thaddean, before he and his

squad lit their jump packs and boosted away from the landing pad. Their guns roared as they sighted more enemies to slaughter.

'And to you, brother,' said Polandrus, igniting his own rockets. He leapt skywards, his brothers close behind, soaring clear of the generatorum and arcing down towards a nearby blockhouse. Polandrus had a fleeting glimpse of the ferrocrete roadway between the two buildings as he passed over it. He spotted more cultists dashing along it, yelling and pointing upwards.

He slammed down on the blockhouse roof. Ahead of him, he saw a bulky flak-cannon emplacement, its barrels aimed at the heavens and a grey-fleshed servitor wired into its flank. With a press of his firing runes, Polandrus annihilated the servitor in a spray of bolts. His brothers added their shots to the fusillade, reducing the anti-aircraft cannon to sparking wreckage.

'Life signs approaching,' said Brother Donadus. 'One floor down.'

'Dispersal pattern,' ordered Polandrus. His battle-brothers redeployed in jet-assisted leaps, forming a semicircle around the exit hatch atop the roof.

The hatch swung open with a clang, and the first cultists spilled upwards. Polandrus had a fleeting impression of rag-wrapped features, yellowed eyes and disease-bloated flesh before the Inceptors blew them apart.

More of the enemy spilled onto the rooftop, only to be blinded by the spraying viscera of their comrades. Bolt shells drilled into their bodies and exploded, slaughtering them wholesale.

'Press the attack,' ordered Polandrus, and he and

his warriors closed up, hosing fire down the stairway below the hatch. Cultists screamed in terror. Most of them died in droves, packed in and unable to escape, before the last of them turned and fled, chased by roaring bolt shells.

'Enough,' said Polandrus. 'Relocate.'

His squad leapt again, dropping from the rooftop of the blockhouse into the square below. Another flak emplacement stood here, surrounded by buildings and flanked by statues of Imperial saints now furred with mould. Polandrus' warriors blitzed the cannon with fire.

'*Gunships inbound,*' voxed Thaddean. Polandrus looked skywards and saw Ultramarines craft sweeping down through the clouds like vengeful angels.

'Three more emplacements to eliminate,' he said. 'Resistance negligible.'

'*Moving on,*' said Thaddean.

At that moment, the distinctive roar of bolters echoed across the square. The shells struck Brother Ulandro, tearing open his chest-plate in a gory spray.

'Death Guard!' roared Brother Donadus, raising his assault bolters and letting fly even as Ulandro's body crashed to the ground.

The Plague Marines strode into the square, bolters up and firing. They were abhorrent, their dirty-green power armour thick with rust and seeping sweat. Gurgling tubes punctured their forms, and plague flies swirled around them.

'Unclean filth!' shouted Sergeant Polandrus, leaping aside on a jet of flame as he opened fire. His shots hammered the nearest Plague Marine, staggering the monstrous warrior and cratering his power armour. Yet the heretic didn't fall, instead giving a gurgling laugh and returning fire.

Bolt shells chased Polandrus through the air, several rounds ricocheting from his armour with punishing force. He landed and leapt again, still firing. More shots struck the trudging Plague Marine, punching through his cracked armour plates and detonating within him. Filthy gore splattered the square as the Death Guard warrior's torso was blown apart.

Still he kept firing.

'Guilliman's oath!' cursed Polandrus. 'These heretics are nigh invulnerable.'

'Enough bolt shells will kill anything, sergeant,' said Donadus fiercely as his stream of shots took off one of the Plague Marines' heads. The heretic's body staggered several more paces, bolter still firing wildly, before toppling onto its side.

'True words, brother,' said Polandrus, unleashing another salvo and snarling in satisfaction as his target finally collapsed, dead.

The last two Plague Marines kept advancing and firing, but they were outmatched. Weathering their fire, the two surviving Inceptors poured shots into the traitors until they were nothing but twitching corpses.

'Heretic filth,' spat Brother Donadus, voice thick with disgust. 'Ulandro was thrice the warrior any of these unworthy things were.'

'Focus, brother,' said Polandrus. 'We will mourn Ulandro later. For now, we have a beachhead to secure.'

Rune-marking the position of Ulandro's fallen body for the Chapter's Apothecaries, Polandrus selected his next target and engaged his jump pack. Meanwhile, the Ultramarines drop-ships swept in to land, shrugging off the last desultory streams of flak fire as they delivered infantry, battle tanks and Dreadnoughts into the fight. The beachhead was as good as secured, and soon the Ultramarines would take the fight to the Death Guard.

In the meantime, Polandrus would avenge his fallen brother in heretic blood.

Far across the city, strange figures stirred within the banquet chamber of a ruined manse. Lithe forms moved through beams of weak daylight, treading with a fluid grace that was entirely alien. The thick dust barely stirred at their passing.

Sat in their midst, their leader raised her head and closed her eyes, reaching out with senses beyond those of the mortal flesh. She breathed deeply, and nodded to herself.

'They have come,' she said, her voice musical and lilting.

She rose from her cross-legged pose, the runes on her armour glowing softly and her long cloak flowing around her like water.

'It is time.'

CHAPTER FOUR

Lieutenant Cassian moved along a roadway between crumbling ruins, bolt rifle sweeping for targets. His strike force was spread through the streets to either side.

Intercessors and Hellblasters jogged from one firing position to the next, stopping to cover their battle-brothers. Aggressors stomped through rubble and ruin, ready to bring point-blank annihilation to anyone that stood in their way. Polandrus' and Thaddean's Inceptors had the flanks, while on high the Reivers of Squad Marcus could be glimpsed as they used grapnel guns to swing from one vantage point to the next, keeping watch for threats.

The strike force's infantry was supported by a pair of Redemptor Dreadnoughts, Brother Indomator and Brother Marius, who strode along in their midst. Fifteen-feet-tall bipedal war engines, each

Dreadnought was built around an armoured sarcoph-agus containing the still-living remains of a mortally wounded battle-brother who piloted his walking tomb as though it were his own body.

Cassian's force was completed by a trio of Repulsor battle tanks, which he had placed at the forefront, an armoured spearhead to drive their attack home. The Repulsors were slab-sided war machines bristling with heavy firepower, hovering several feet off the ground on thrumming grav-fields that would crush and pum-mel anything they passed over, be it rubble, wreckage or enemies.

'Chaplain Dematris?' voxed Cassian.

'No resistance yet,' replied Dematris from his position one street over. *'The enemy clearly lack fortitude, or else they would come and oppose us.'*

'If there is one thing the Death Guard do not lack, it is fortitude,' said Keritraeus from his position elsewhere on the line. *'We are making good progress, but we should remain cautious.'*

'The foe should not be underestimated,' agreed Cassian. 'But we captured our beachhead with virtually no casualties, and we still have the element of surprise. With luck, we will reach our objective before they can rally more than token forces against us.'

'We also have the Primarch's Sword,' added Dematris. *'Shipmaster Aethor has enough weapons systems working to provide a substantial planetary bombardment should it be required.'*

'The tainted atmospherics render auspex scans unrelia-ble,' said Keritraeus. *'We do not know for sure where our enemies are. We have only ghost returns.'*

'What do you counsel?' asked Cassian.

'We slow our advance. We use the Reivers to scout the path ahead. If we cannot rely on the senses of our machine-spirits, then we must instead rely upon our own.'

'An excess of caution,' said Dematris. *'Surprise is an advantage that lasts only so long. Everything we know of the Death Guard suggests that they are predominately an infantry force, exceptionally resilient and deadly in close-range firefights, but ponderous. If we give them time to respond, the situation will deteriorate rapidly.'*

'Lieutenant, I cannot agree,' said Keritraeus. *'The enemy has been here for weeks. With the auspex so unreliable, we have no way of knowing where their forces might be massed. And they are still Space Marines, let us not forget. I believe it would be a grave error to rush blindly in on the assumption that they did not have contingencies in place for just such an attack.'*

'Brothers, I hear you both,' said Cassian, 'but I must err on the side of decisive action, for every moment spent away from the primarch's side is a moment we are failing in our duty. However, I agree that we must determine our foe's true location and strength. That is why we require more eyes on the ground. Eyes that I intend to secure now.'

So saying, he cut the link to his brothers and began to cycle methodically through Imperial command channels, sending out a rune-coded interrogation to each one.

Cassian led his Intercessors across a rubble-strewn intersection, stepping around collected pools of oily filth. It had begun to rain, a light, greasy drizzle whose touch Cassian did not trust – wary of heretical contaminants, he had ordered his brothers to keep their helms on. He ducked through a blackened archway and picked his way through the bombed-out ruin of a hab-block. Heaps of remains lay rotting here, the sad remnants of Dustrious' inhabitants now little more than fly-picked bones.

As Cassian emerged into daylight again, he saw the astropathic fortress standing proud on a hilltop in the middle distance. According to his helm's auto-senses, the structure now lay just a few miles ahead. At the Space Marines' swift pace, they would reach it in less than twenty minutes. If the enemy had not made themselves known by then, he would use the fortress as his base of operations and begin hunting the heretics while he waited for the Indomitus Crusade fleet's response to his astropathic message.

Cassian's vox crackled. A coded response came back to him, indicating a secure channel.

'This is Lieutenant Cassian Talasadian of the Ultramarines Fourth Company,' said Cassian. 'Identify yourself in the Emperor's name.'

'My lord, it is good to hear your voice,' came the reply. *'This is Captain Dzansk, Cadian Forty-Fourth Heavy Infantry.'*

Cassian heard exhaustion in the man's voice, along with an unhealthy hoarseness, but also steel.

Cadian, he thought. They were the most renowned of all the Astra Militarum's countless regiments, and arguably the finest.

'Captain Dzansk, well met,' said Cassian. 'Appraise me of your disposition.'

'I am the surviving ranking officer in the Dustrious

warzone,' said Dzansk. *'From an initial regimental strength of five thousand men and two hundred armoured vehicles, I currently command eight hundred and twenty-two able-bodied men and women of Cadia, along with seventeen Leman Russ battle tanks and twenty-one Chimeras. We are operating out of the Temple District, where we have fortified several structures. Ammunition is low, and rations and medicae supplies virtually nil. Sickness is rife and morale has been steadily deteriorating. Though if I may say so, my lord, your arrival will do much to bring heart to my soldiers.'*

'How long have you been in the field?' asked Cassian. 'And what can you tell me about the enemy here? Strengths, dispositions, capabilities?'

'They attacked twenty-one days ago,' said Dzansk. *'Bombarded the city from orbit with viral contaminants and conventional ordnance. We lost over half the regiment during that first attack. I and a few other officers managed to get our troops to the shelters, but the rest... After that, the Death Guard landed a force of – I would estimate – two to three hundred Heretic Astartes supported by war machines and heavy mobile artillery. General Yorin attempted a counter-attack in force, but the contagions the enemy had dropped made the battlefield hazardous. Worse, many citizens and soldiers who fell to their plagues rose up again as revenants and overran our lines.'*

Cassian frowned, disturbed by the estimated enemy numbers. There were more heretics here than orbital scans suggested.

'The counter-offensive failed utterly, my lord,' continued Dzansk. *'It cost us at least another thousand able bodies, along with Yorin and his entire upper command staff. My*

men and I have been holding out ever since, attempting to harass the enemy wherever possible, and launching meas-ured attacks to break their besiegement of the astropathic fortress. Thus far we have met with only defeat. I believe we have endured this long only because the enemy do not fight as a sane man would, instead seeking to draw out our misery for as long as they can.'

'You have done what you could, and the Emperor will look kindly upon you for it,' said Cassian. 'Now, however, He has a different duty for you, captain.'

'Of course, my lord. What are your orders?'

'My brothers and I are pushing towards the astro-pathic fortress. We must secure it in order to despatch a message to the Indomitus Crusade. We must rejoin our comrades and free the stars from the rule of Chaos.'

'A crusade?' asked Dzansk, excitement in his voice. *'My lord, we had no idea. We thought, perhaps…'*

'That it was the end?' said Cassian. 'No, captain, this is just the beginning of the heretics' final defeat. But in order to play our part in that battle, we must return to our comrades. Aid us in that fight, and the Emperor will smile upon you. Guilliman needs all the warriors he can get.'

'Guilliman?' asked Dzansk, his Cadian discipline slip-ping for a moment. *'My lord?'*

'Our father has returned to us,' said Cassian. 'There is much to tell, captain, but it can wait. For now, I need you to mobilise your forces and support our advance.'

'At once, my lord. Send me your coordinates, and I will mobilise the regiment.'

Cassian tapped the runes on his vambrace, each one flashing briefly and fading again as he despatched the data to the auspex-inload channel Dzansk provided. There was a pause, then Dzansk spoke again, his voice urgent.

'My lord, you are well within Death Guard territory. They have maintained their perimeter around the fortress at a remove of between three and five miles since their siege began. They have some sorcery that shields them from our auspex. You should have had some engagement by now. If you haven't seen them yet, it's because–'

'They know we're coming,' said Cassian.

Lord Gurloch stood still as a statue on the ground floor of a skeletal ruin. Every inch of his armour was covered with fat-bodied plague flies whose only movement was a slight riffling of their wings. Blorthos' Blightlord Terminators stood around him, each with their own coating of bloated insects. Beyond the ruin, Gurloch's forces spread away to either flank, forming a long, deep battle-line utterly carpeted in plague flies.

No one moved.

The vox was silent.

The ambush was ready.

Gurloch saw the first flash of blue armour through the greasy drizzle. A tall, clean-limbed loyalist, different to any he had seen before, picked his way through the ruins as he swept left and right with a long-barrelled bolt weapon.

Then came another one, and another. The Murmuring Swarm had concealed Gurloch and his warriors from the enemy's auspex, but any second now they would make visual contact. It was time.

'In the name of Mortarion and the Grandfather,' said Gurloch over the vox, 'begin the attack.'

As one, a billion flies lifted off from the Death Guard warriors and swarmed into the air with a thunderous droning. In the same instant, Gurloch's warriors raised their guns, bellowed gargling war cries and attacked.

Gurloch himself stomped through the crumbled ruins of a low wall, crushing the rubble to dust. Around him, the Blightlord Terminators opened fire. Their shots blitzed the Ultramarines' front line, bolts sparking from blue power armour and gouts of plague-ridden filth sizzling as they ate through adamantium and ceramite.

The Ultramarines responded with commendable speed, and Gurloch was surprised to see just how resilient they were. The warriors took shots to their torsos, helms and limbs, some of which even punched through their armour and blasted bloody craters in their flesh, but they still returned fire, hammering volleys of bolts into their ambushers. Gurloch heard one of the Witherlings grunt in pain as a shot found a weak spot in his armour, blowing a bucketful of greasy pus across the walls.

Shots spanged off Gurloch's breastplate, and he gave a wet laugh.

'You will have to do better than that, little brothers!' he roared. 'Your Corpse-Emperor is nothing compared to the might of Nurgle. Come, let me bathe you in the generosity of my god!'

Crashing through another wall, Gurloch shrugged off the hammering fire of the nearest Ultramarine and swung his plaguereaper in a mighty arc. The axe was as tall as a grown man, and had three buzz-saw blades mounted within its cutting edge, forming the tri-lobed sigil of Nurgle. Those blades howled as they cut through the Ultramarine's chest-plate, scything in under his left arm and tearing out under his right.

The Ultramarine staggered, blood jetting from the catastrophic wound in his torso. Chuckling, Gurloch levelled his axe and smashed its head like a spear into his enemy's faceplate. Ceramite crumpled, eye-lenses shattered, and the butchered Space Marine crashed onto his back.

Another Ultramarines warrior came at Gurloch, hurling a primed krak grenade at him. The implosive charge struck his shoulder and detonated, crumpling rusted armour and tearing through rotten flesh. Gurloch growled in pain as foul fluids and gobbets of fat drizzled from the wound. The Ultramarine pressed forwards, drawing a bolt pistol and firing it point-blank into Gurloch's face.

The shot rebounded from his helm, rocking his head back, but the Lord of Contagion rallied with a roar of anger.

'You slopsome little slug!' he bellowed. 'You think that the sons of Mortarion fall so easily, do you?'

Swatting the Ultramarine's pistol aside, Gurloch grabbed his assailant around the throat and hefted him high. He brought the revving blades of his plaguereaper up and rammed them into the Ultramarine's midriff, ripping through power armour and churning into the flesh beneath. His victim roared in agony as he was disembowelled, limbs spasming and dancing. The Space Marine managed to ball a fist and drive it into Gurloch's faceplate once, then twice. The third swing had no strength behind it, and then he was nothing but dead meat.

Gurloch tossed his enemy aside, glancing at the wound already sucking closed in his shoulder. Thick tentacles squirmed from his skin and wove together, secreting a slimy gruel that rapidly hardened into chitinous plates. Small yellow eyes rose like blisters upon the unnatural skin, bursting open with little fluid pops.

Gurloch laughed and raised his head to the sky as, all around him, his warriors pressed home their ambush against the Imperial lapdogs.

'Thank you, great Nurgle!' cried Gurloch. 'Thank you for your blessings! We offer you tribute in return!'

Cassian ducked behind a wall, feeling it shudder as bolt shells slammed into it. Stone shrapnel flew, and flies boiled around him in a blinding cloud.

He ducked out from cover, firing his bolt rifle on full-auto. His shots slammed into the nearest Plague Marine, blasting a rent in the traitor's chest-plate and another in his helm. The Plague Marine staggered, but stayed on his feet and kept firing.

'Emperor curse their unholy resilience,' said Cassian. 'Sergeant Gallen, illuminate them please.'

'At once, brother-lieutenant,' replied Gallen. From across the courtyard, a salvo of sun-bright plasma slammed into the Plague Marines as Gallen's Hellblasters let fly. Volley after searing volley struck home, melting power armour, vaporising fluids and blasting diseased flesh to ashes. The Plague Marines died to a man, their fused remains tangled together in a heap.

'Magnificent, brother,' said Cassian. 'Thank you.'

'We do the primarch's work,' said Gallen. 'But we will need a moment – our guns' machine-spirits become enraged to excess. They must cool.'

'Understood. Fall back and have Sergeant Emastus' Hellblasters take your place. Circle around to Librarian Keritraeus' position and reinforce against the push in that sector.'

'At once, brother-lieutenant,' said Gallen, and his men bore their glowing weapons away towards the rear lines.

'Dematris,' voxed Cassian, 'how do you fare?'

'They press hard,' came the reply. Cassian heard the crackle of the Chaplain's crozius arcanum in the background, and the sounds of rattling bolt fire. *'But we shall not yield! Dreadnought-Brother Indomator is holding them back, and I have despatched squads Telor and Adamastes to work around the flank and provide enfilading fire.'*

'We will enfold the edge of their ambushing force and turn their flank,' said Cassian, 'then break through with the Aggressors. That will allow us to stall their momentum and regain our own.'

'Lieutenant,' voxed Keritraeus. *'We've lost one of our Repulsors.* Onslaught Intractable *was struck from both flanks by armour-piercing projectiles. It's a wreck.'*

'Damn,' said Cassian under his breath. 'What of *Maximus' Revenge* and *Pride of Talassar*?'

'Both still fighting, brother,' said Keritraeus. *'I've ordered them to pull back and stabilise our line. The enemy advance in dominant numbers, and they simply refuse to die.'*

'Here too,' said Cassian. 'I've sent you a squad of

Hellblasters to help with that. Dematris is preparing a counter-attack on his flank. We need to hold our ground long enough for him to drive it home.'

'*Respectfully, I'm not sure that's wise, brother-lieutenant,*' replied Keritraeus. '*The enemy surprised us. They outnumber and outgun us. Retreat would be the wiser option.*'

'If Dematris' attack fails, then I will give the order. But we *must* try. Duty compels us.'

'*Wisdom is not cowardice, brother, but I bow to your authority.*'

Cassian leaned out from cover and fired again, severing a Plague Marine's leg at the knee. He ducked back as ferocious return fire hammered his position.

'Captain Dzansk,' he said, switching channels. 'Are you in position to reinforce?'

'*Negative, my lord,*' replied Dzansk. '*Our enemy planned his ambush well – we're dealing with an attack of our own here. If I send forces to your position, I will irreparably weaken my own.*'

'Understood. Hold out. Survive. When we break these heretic curs, we will require your forces for the counterpunch.'

'*Yes, my lord,*' said Dzansk, and cut the link.

Cassian checked his auspex and scowled. Death Guard runes swarmed his forward positions, outnumbering his forces by a substantial margin. However, he had his duty, and the blood of Guilliman running through his veins. He was determined that no heretic would defeat him.

With a quick flurry of runic commands, Cassian ordered Aggressor squads Temeter and Doras forward on the left, and called Intercessor squad Latreaus up to his position. His brothers raised their bolt rifles as he led them out across the courtyard, pouring fire into the Plague Marines in the ruins on the other side.

A sudden scream filled the air, swelling to deafening proportions. Cassian saw shells dropping through the fly-thick air.

'Incoming!' he yelled. 'Disperse!'

His men leapt to obey, flinging themselves aside as the huge shells crashed down upon the courtyard. They detonated, hurling warriors through the air and throwing Cassian backwards through a stained-glass window.

He staggered to his feet, ears ringing, and stared through the shattered remains of the window at the slaughter before him. The shells had disgorged swirling clouds of black spores that were dissolving everything they touched. Intercessors writhed and choked as their armour, flesh and bone were eaten away. The ruins themselves began to crumble and dissolve, and the ground tipped as the spores chewed a deep crater in the earth.

Cassian scrambled back, diving through an arched doorway as the courtyard and the ruins around it fell away into the pit. He cursed the reckless insanity of his foes, to hurl such inimical munitions into the midst of a point-blank firefight. His fury became horror as he heard the rolling boom of another barrage being fired from behind the Death Guard lines, then another.

Huge shells rained down along the Ultramarines line, vomiting fire and spore clouds.

'*Lieutenant Cassian,*' voxed Dematris. '*Squad Telor is all but annihilated, and Sergeant Adamastes is pulling his* surviving battle-brothers back. We cannot endure in the face of such firepower.'

'Lieutenant,' said Keritraeus a moment later, 'I am doing what I can to shield our brothers with the force of my mind, but those shells are death incarnate. If we don't do something quickly, we're going to be shelled into oblivion!'

'Brother-lieutenant,' voxed Reiver Sergeant Marcus, 'the enemy are moving industrial track units around the flanks. They're carrying iron cages the size of Thunderhawk gunships. Throne, they're full of... They're hard to identify – humanoid, mutant-like characteristics, packed in like livestock and groaning like the damned.'

'Our enemy mean to pen us in with these creatures and then finish us off with shelling and gunfire,' Cassian said as the artillery boomed again. 'Primarch, forgive me. This isn't a battle. I've led us into a massacre...'

CHAPTER FIVE

The rain fell harder. It hissed against ferrocrete and drew oily streaks down the Ultramarines' power armour. A chorus of groans echoed through the ruins as hundreds of plague mutants spilled from their cages and shambled towards Guilliman's sons. Shells screamed like daemons as they plunged down into the battle, and the Death Guard pressed their attack.

Cassian slid Duty from its sheath. He pressed his thumb against the sword's activation rune, and a field of crackling power leapt up its blade.

'Emperor and primarch hear my oath,' he said as the Plague Marines lumbered closer through the rain. 'I will not let my brothers die here. I will not sacrifice them upon the altar of my ambition. Lend me strength – I shall pay whatever price I must.'

Lunging from cover, Cassian drove his blade through the gut of the closest heretic. He ripped the weapon free in a shower of foul viscera, and his victim crashed to his knees.

Cassian staggered as a second Plague Marine shot him point-blank, cratering his chest-plate and cracking the black carapace that fused his power armour to his body.

Rallying, the lieutenant placed a bolt through his attacker's right eye-lens, blowing out the back of the Plague Marine's head. He then spun around and under an axe swing that would have cut him in half, before lopping the third Plague Marine's arm from his shoulder.

Cassian's enemy gave a gurgle of anger, seeming not to feel the wound. The Plague Marine swung again, one-handed, but Cassian parried before ramming Duty point first through the traitor's throat.

The Plague Marine sagged as fluids pumped from his ruined neck, but still he took another swing that almost connected with Cassian's chest. Angrily, the lieutenant ripped his blade free and swept it in a killing arc to remove the Plague Marine's helm from his shoulders.

'Stay dead, filth,' spat Cassian as his enemy crumpled.

'Brother-lieutenant,' came Dematris' voice over the vox, 'they're outflanking us, but with zeal we can still prevail! I shall rally my forces and lead them in a counter-attack.'

'No,' said Cassian firmly. 'We serve no one by dying here for nothing.'

'Not for nothing,' said Dematris angrily. 'For vengeance! For ten thousand years of wrongdoing! What is the crusade, if not a war of revenge? We don't need to rejoin the primarch to claim that – there are plenty of foes before us.'

'The crusade is a war of unity,' said Cassian. 'It is the primarch's quest to drive back the shadow of Chaos from the Emperor's realm. We are part of that quest. We are his weapons, and I guarantee you that Lord Guilliman has a better use for us than to see us blunted and ruined on this backwater.'

Dematris gave a grunt of acknowledgement. It was enough.

'Lieutenant,' voxed Keritraeus, *'what is our plan? We are mired in the living dead here, and we will soon be overrun.'*

Cassian thought furiously, knowing he had moments to act. He heard the scream of incoming ordnance, and saw the heavy shells slam down in the ruins to his right. Spores billowed.

'Dematris, Keritraeus,' he voxed. 'Pull your battle-brothers back and find what cover you can. Regroup and be ready to fall back.'

'Lieutenant,' said Keritraeus urgently, *'if we close ranks they'll kill us all the quicker.'*

'They're not the only ones with ordnance to deploy,' said Cassian, before switching vox-channels. 'Shipmaster Aethor, this is Lieutenant Cassian.'

'I hear you, my lord,' came Aethor's clipped tones.

'Aethor, can you pinpoint the position of the enemy batteries?'

'Within a quarter mile. No closer. The storm, my lord.'

'It will do,' said Cassian. 'On my order, fire a spread of orbital torpedoes at the enemy artillery's position, then commence a creeping barrage of lance fire towards our own. Stop only when you reach us.'

'Our efforts will be inaccurate, lord,' said Aethor.

'Do what you can. The Emperor expects.'

'Understood, my lord.'

'Be ready, brothers,' said Cassian, addressing the strike force. 'Sergeant Marcus, get your Reivers clear. Everyone else, brace for barrage shock.'

Vox-pips and confirmation runes flashed back to him as his warriors continued to lay down fire into their attackers. Cassian saw corpse-like figures stumbling through the rain towards him. Dozens of them. Hundreds. A shambling wall of diseased flesh and mutant appendages, their rictus grins and staring eyes burning themselves into his memory.

High above, he could see black specks plunge through the clouds, driven groundwards on trails of flame. This was going to be close.

'Emperor, shield your servants from harm,' he said, firing his bolt rifle into the horde before ducking behind the rusting wreck of a cargo transport.

The orbital torpedoes struck. The first sign was a searing brightness, a false dawn that threw hard-edged shadows across the ruins. Then came the sound, a mounting roar accompanied by a hammer blow of hyperbaric shock. If Cassian's power armour hadn't protected him, his lungs would have been torn out through his throat by the sudden pressure wave and his flesh seared from his bones by the roiling firestorm.

The wreck was plucked up and hurled through the air, taking Cassian with it. He had a fleeting impression of towering blast clouds rising above the cityscape, perhaps a mile to the north, and of the mangled remains of diseased corpses scattering like fleshy rain.

Then Cassian hit the ground, and the cargo transport slammed down on top of him.

Dim light.

The flickering of electrical input and runic signals.

Dull chatter, resolving itself slowly into distinct voices. His brothers' voices.

Cassian opened his eyes and assessed the damage. His auto-senses were flashing with amber and red hazard runes. He couldn't move.

It took Cassian a moment to realise that he was pinned firmly under the wreck of the cargo hauler, with only his head and one arm protruding. He gasped a breath and flexed his fingers, straining to reach Duty, but the power sword's hilt was just out of reach.

He pushed, trying to lift the wreck off himself. Fibre-bundles in his armour flexed, lending their strength to his own. He snarled with effort as the wreck shifted and slowly rose – one inch, two, *three*. Yet the weight was just too much, even for one of the Emperor's finest, and the wreck thumped back down. Cassian hissed with pain.

Macabre remains lay in piles of corpse-meat around him, much of it still twitching. He grunted as he saw a half-figure tumble from the nearest pile and start dragging itself towards him using the hilt of a shattered sword. Perhaps the thing had once been a manufactorum worker, or maybe a militiaman; now it was nothing but rotting flesh, blackened overalls and grinning, pointed teeth growing closer by the moment. More came behind it, tumbling from the heaps like maggots and dragging themselves in his direction, groaning.

Cassian snarled, preparing to fight off these carrion things. In honest combat, the creatures would barely have given him pause, but with his body trapped and many of the undead mutants armed? Those blades would punch through an eye-lens or saw through the neck seal of his helm eventually.

He opened a vox-channel to call for help, but before he could speak a huge ceramite foot slammed down on the leading mutant and crushed it.

'Up you come, brother-lieutenant,' boomed a vox-amplified voice. 'You'll be no use commanding from under that wreck.'

Cassian looked up at Brother Marius. The Redemptor Dreadnought's blue armour had been scorched black by the blasts and dented by numerous impacts, yet Marius seemed none the worse for wear. With a whine of servos, he reached down and gripped the wreck with his articulated power fist. Metal crumpled in the Dreadnought's grasp, and he hefted the remains of the cargo transport off Cassian as easily as though it were made of parchment.

As the wreck crashed onto its side, Cassian got to his feet. His Mark X Tacticus power armour was battered and rent in several places, and he could barely move his left arm, but he was alive.

'Brother, my thanks,' he said.

'Lead us on to victory, and we will call it even,' boomed the Dreadnought. He pivoted on his waist gimbal, and Cassian's audio-dampers cut in as Marius' heavy onslaught Gatling cannon screamed into life. Rounds blitzed the ruins to their right, and Plague Marines died in eruptions of gore.

'*Cassian?*' came Keritraeus' voice over the vox. '*Brother-lieutenant, respond.*'

'Here, Keritraeus,' said Cassian. High above, the clouds were lit crimson as a lance of laser energy stabbed down. A ruin a hundred yards north shuddered then collapsed as the blast ripped through it.

'*Lieutenant, the enemy is scattered, shell-shocked, but so are we. That was reckless.*'

'It was necessary,' said Cassian, before switching channels to address his entire force. 'Brothers,' he said, 'pull back now. Fighting retreat to these coordinates.'

Runes flashed back. Several sergeants warned that their battle-brothers were scattered, still recovering from the first barrage.

Some didn't reply at all.

Crimson light pierced the clouds again as the *Primarch's Sword* dropped another lance blast into the combat zone. The explosion shook the ground beneath Cassian's feet. Yet he knew the risk was worth it, for his enemy possessed greater numbers and would be suffering far worse against such a bombardment.

'Dematris, Keritraeus,' he voxed, 'lead the retreat. I will rally those squads still pinned. Captain Dzansk, my men are going to fall back towards your stronghold. Be ready to receive us.'

A Plague Marine appeared through the swirling smoke and dust and rain. Marius' cannon cut him to gory chunks.

'*That will not be necessary, lieutenant,*' came a lilting voice over the vox. Cassian frowned as he saw a channel he didn't recognise flash up on his auto-senses.

'Identify,' he barked. 'Are you with Dzansk?'

'*Prepare to extract your remaining warriors,*' said the unknown speaker. '*Fall back to these coordinates. Make haste.*'

'Identify,' repeated Cassian as a runic waypoint flashed up on his helm auspex. 'Or is this just another machination of the foe?'

'*Our enemies are the same, Lieutenant Cassian, even if our species differ.*'

'*Lieutenant,*' said Keritraeus. '*I'm sensing a prodigious psychic build-up. Something is coming.*'

Before Cassian's eyes, the rain slowed and hung in place, forming a glittering veil of impossible droplets. The air stilled. The drone of flies and the roar of gunfire became muted.

A sudden hurricane of psychic energy tore through the air. The halted downpour whipped outwards, caught in the ferocity of a storm that swept up debris, corpses and wreckage and hurled them towards the Death Guard lines.

Cassian's eyes widened as he realised the storm had left him and Marius untouched.

'*Lieutenant, this isn't my doing,*' voxed Keritraeus. '*It has the feel of xenos rune-craft. But if ever we needed something to cover our retreat…*'

'Agreed,' said Cassian, making a snap decision. 'All battle-brothers, fall back on these coordinates. Be swift, but be wary.'

Cassian sheathed his blade and jogged back through the ruins, reloading his bolt rifle despite his wounded arm. Marius thumped along beside him as the psychic tempest continued to hurl corpses and rubble through the air, driving the Death Guard back with its battering onslaught.

Sorcery heaped on sorcery. A swift and simple offensive had become a convoluted and costly battle.

Cassian would have answers.

The rendezvous point was a bombed-out cathedrum, located two miles east of Captain Dzansk's position. The blasted structure was still magnificent for all its battle damage. Saints stared down from stained-glass windows, while gothic spires stabbed up into the clouds like rain-slick daggers.

As Cassian and Marius approached through rubble and wreckage, more Ultramarines appeared through the rain to join them. The lieutenant saw others waiting outside the cathedrum, and noted that they had their weapons levelled at the structure.

Keritraeus and Dematris came to Cassian's side as he neared the building. Both were battered and scorched, but appeared uninjured.

'Cassian, auspex shows multiple life signs within the cathedrum. Approximately twenty – xenos,' said Dematris. 'We felt it best to wait for your arrival before deciding how to proceed.'

'That psychic event struck the entire battle front,' said Keritraeus. 'It persisted for almost ten minutes after the last battle-brothers disengaged. Cassian, the psychic fortitude it would take to manifest such a phenomenon is staggering. We may be dealing with an entire conclave of witches. These mysterious allies could be every bit as dangerous as the enemies we have just escaped.'

'I don't believe they are a danger,' said Cassian. 'Not to us, at least.'

'It was a storm of their raising that covered our retreat,' admitted Dematris, 'but the works of aliens are unclean. They cannot be trusted, nor treated with lightly.'

'In this I must agree with Dematris,' said Keritraeus. 'Clearly these xenos mean us no immediate harm, otherwise they simply would have allowed the Death Guard to overwhelm us. But neither would they aid us out of simple charity. Their very being here seems too convenient for mere chance.'

'They knew me,' said Cassian. 'The one that addressed me did so by name and rank. Maintain a cordon and have Apothecary Lamdas see to the wounded. Keritraeus, contact Captain Dzansk and establish the status of his forces. I am going to speak to our mysterious allies.'

'You are wounded yourself, brother-lieutenant,' said Keritraeus. 'Lamdas should inspect that arm, if nothing else.'

'After,' said Cassian, then turned away and strode up the cathedrum steps.

The interior of the building was thick with shadows and whirling dust, yet he could feel the aliens' piercing gaze. Cassian kept his hands well away from his weapons, walking forwards slowly and deliberately as he swept the cavernous structure with his auto-senses.

'Make yourselves known,' he called, his voice echoing into the gloom. 'You told me to come here. I have come. Now reveal yourselves in the Emperor's name, and state your purpose.'

'Our purpose?' The reply drifted from the shadows, whispering around him like a wind. The voice was musical, lilting. Female, he thought. 'Lieutenant Cassian, the true answer to that question would be more than even your transhuman mind could comprehend. But put simply? Our purpose is survival.'

Cassian was deep within the cathedrum now, surrounded by shadows, rubble and the looming silhouettes of old altars and statuary. Amidst the darkness, he caught movement in his peripheral vision: lithe figures in slender, sculpted armour and elongated helms were moving to surround him, chainsword-analogues and alien pistols poised.

'You are aeldari,' said Cassian, halting his advance. 'Craftworlders? How does preventing our defeat aid your survival? How do you know me?'

'Your kind are normally so closed-minded,' said the voice, a slight edge of mockery in its tone. 'Yet *you* have so many questions.'

'This is not a game,' said Cassian angrily. 'Good battle-brothers fell today, and their deaths are upon my conscience. My enemies seem insurmountable, yet my duty is inescapable. And now you appear with aid unsought, calling me by name and unleashing powers that my Librarian assures me are monumental in scope. Yes, I have questions, and I would have you provide answers, or by Macragge and Ultramar I will order my men to bring this roof down with all of us inside.'

'That would be… unwise, lieutenant,' said the voice. Something flew out of the darkness and clattered at Cassian's feet. He recoiled, drawing Duty in an instant and scanning for threats.

The xenos warriors remained unmoving. Cassian realised that the object now lying at his feet was a tall staff, graven from a bone-like substance and decorated with xenoform runes. It was lined with gems, all blackened and cracked, and silvery smoke drifted from a much larger gem held in a setting at its end.

'The Dreamer's Stave,' said the voice. 'An ancient relic of my people that had endured since before your kind lost its first empire amongst the stars. I destroyed it unleashing the conjuration that saved you and your warriors from death. I trust that the seriousness of this sacrifice indicates my own.'

'I have only your word for this,' said Cassian, 'but let us suppose for now that I am convinced.'

He stayed still, aware of the xenos warriors' eyes upon him as the speaker emerged from the shadows. She was tall and willow-thin, her armour and robes flowing around her like silk in a breeze. An ornate blade was fastened at her hip, and she went unhelmed, her features angular, sculpted and inescapably alien. She stopped before Cassian, the ruined stave lying between them, and fixed him with her amber eyes.

'I am Farseer Ithlae, of Craftworld Yme'Loc,' she said. 'I know you, Lieutenant Cassian, because I have foreseen all of this in the runes.'

Cassian framed his next question carefully.

'If you were able to predict all of this,' he began, 'then why not simply intercede before the battle began? If you wished to aid us, why not forewarn us of the ambush? Lives could have been saved.'

'Lieutenant, your lives mean less than nothing to me. Furthermore, fate is... You might envision it as a river.

It can be dammed, its course altered, but one must be careful when doing so, lest the river burst its banks or take a path other than the one you sought. The dam must be placed at precisely the correct intersection to change the flow as desired, or all is for naught. The moment that your defeat drew nigh – *that* was the perfect intersection.'

Cassian restrained his building anger, but his hands tightened into fists.

'You will next ask me why I did not bring a greater force,' continued the farseer, 'or perhaps why I chose a path that necessitated the ruin of such a precious and ancient artefact. I will endeavour to explain the price that must be paid to alter fate, at which point you will have still more questions for which I cannot provide you with explanations that your crude psyche can comprehend. And all the while, our mutual enemy rallies his strength.'

'Speak your piece, then,' said Cassian. 'You save us, and say you did so to aid your own survival. Why? What do you expect in return? What threat are the Death Guard to you?'

The farseer gave a lilting laugh both musical and deeply unsettling.

'These plague-ridden vermin? No, lieutenant, the Death Guard pose no threat to Yme'Loc. At least not here. Not now.'

'Then what–'

'*You*, lieutenant,' said Ithlae, cutting off his next question. 'It is my duty to save you. Specifically. In days not yet dawned, your deeds will save us in kind. You will fight for Craftworld Yme'Loc, and thus you yourself must survive to fulfil your destiny.'

'Foolishness,' said Cassian, incredulous. 'I know our species have found tenuous ground for alliance when we must, but I am no xenophile. I would no more fight for a craftworld than I would to protect an ork warlord or defend a necron tomb! You have wasted your time, farseer, if you think that I will barter my loyalty for my continued survival.'

'I did not say that you would *intentionally* fight for us, lieutenant,' replied Ithlae. 'It is already done. Your feet are on the path. By living to fight another day, you have defied the end that fate laid out for you. You walk in our webs now.'

Cassian felt horrified anger rise within him. His hand gripped Duty's hilt.

'Lies! My life is not lived in thrall to some xenos witch!'

'Believe what you will,' said the farseer dismissively. 'You asked, and I answered. It is nothing to me if you accept the truth. Whatever the case, we must take our leave, for you still have a battle to fight, and we wish no further part in it.'

'Cowards,' spat Cassian.

'A last word of advice, lieutenant. Remember that your enemies here do not think as you do. To one who has sold their soul to Chaos, madness seems like logic. Consider that your enemy's strength may also be his weakness, his faith also his curse.'

'I have warriors all around this structure. Do not think you can simply dismiss us so easily, xenos. You will remain and answer to me.'

'No, lieutenant,' said the farseer with a faint smile, 'I will not.'

The aeldari faded back into the shadows. Cassian followed, casting caution aside as he sought to keep the xenos in his sights. He barked orders through the vox, commanding his battle-brothers to stand ready and apprehend all aeldari forces emerging from the cathedrum, and for several squads to converge on his position and help him sweep the ruined building.

It was only minutes later, with the xenos vanished and no sign of them reported either within the cathedrum or without, that Cassian was forced to admit the truth: the aeldari had disappeared as mysteriously as they appeared.

They were gone, leaving only questions in their wake.

CHAPTER SIX

'Squad Polandrus reports no signs of pursuit by the Death Guard,' said Dematris.

He and Keritraeus stood on the steps of the ruined cathedrum, staring out into the rain-slick ruins. Their brothers maintained a perimeter, Intercessors and Hellblasters standing guard while the wounded were seen to and Techmarine Tyvos repaired the strike force's remaining Repulsor battle tanks.

'That's the last squad to report in,' replied the Librarian. 'The heretics chose not to drive home their attack.'

'Perhaps they lack the proper zeal,' said Dematris. 'Between Shipmaster Aethor's bombardment and the storm raised by that xenos witch, the traitors may have been put to flight.'

'Perhaps, but the Death Guard pride themselves on their capacity to endure. I doubt we broke their nerve, brother.'

'Whatever the case, the respite is welcome. Time for us to regroup and rearm, to focus ourselves and prepare for the next attack.'

'Time enough, also, to scout the lie of the land, and attempt to coordinate more closely with our allies,' said Keritraeus. 'Squads Marcus, Polandrus and Thaddean make good progress.'

'Have you had any success reaching the astropathic conclave inside the fortress?' asked Dematris, methodically checking over his plasma pistol's workings.

Keritraeus shook his head in frustration.

'Nothing,' he said. 'The warp is agitated, and the presence of the Death Guard worsens things. But I ought to be able to sense something there. I have tried repeatedly to project my thoughts into their own, but it is as though they simply are not there.'

'I know little of witchery. Does that mean they're dead? Do we fight for naught?'

'I don't know, brother. Perhaps. Or maybe they have hidden their minds somehow, the better to survive the heretical forces beyond their walls. Until we gain entry to the astropathic fortress, I fear it will remain a mystery.'

'Then let's hope the lieutenant emerges from his meditations soon,' said Dematris. 'I am keen to extract vengeance for those we lost today.'

'As are we all, brother,' agreed Keritraeus. 'But have a little patience. Cassian has much to think on, and he cannot risk another defeat.'

'Every minute the foe remains unprosecuted risks defeat. If he does not emerge soon, I will rouse him myself. There's a war to be won.'

Cassian was deep within the ruins of the cathedrum. He had found a small annex that remained untouched by the destruction. Its stained-glass triptychs were intact, and its devotional candles stood in their mounts as though waiting for a priest to come and light them. Cassian had taken this as a sign, and chosen to make his devotions here.

The lieutenant's injured arm had been temporarily freed from its sheath of power armour. It was encased instead in a gelid medi-compress that flooded the limb with hypernutrients and muscle stimms to aid recovery. Ignoring the stinging discomfort, Cassian knelt unhelmed before the spread wings of a golden aquila. Duty's point was driven into the tile floor, and his forehead rested against its pommel.

He had knelt like this now for over an hour, attempting to still his thoughts and meditate upon all that had occurred. At first his mind had whirled with frustration and anger, his hatred for the traitors only marginally less than his disgust at himself.

Then there was the deep sense of disquiet that the farseer's words had brought him. Cassian was a Primaris Space Marine, one of Archmagos Cawl's original warriors who had stepped directly from stasis and taken up arms during the Ultima Founding. Ingrained into every fibre of his being was a sense of purpose and duty, a certainty that his every thought and deed served the Imperium of Mankind. It was, in a very literal sense, what he had been created for.

That certainty had been shaken, first by his defeat at the hands of the Death Guard, then by the aeldari's intimation that he now walked their path. Cassian was unused to the idea that his fate lay in anyone's hands but the Emperor's.

He found himself scrutinising his every thought, deed and utterance.

Space Marines were not religious in the way that most Imperial servants were; they did not, as a rule, deify the Emperor, nor pray to Him for direct intercession. Yet they were still deeply spiritual beings in their own way, venerating their primarchs and their Emperor, and deriving strength from their examples.

It was this that had allowed Cassian to finally calm his mind, to centre his thoughts and slip into a meditative state during which he had dissected every fragment of information he had gathered, analysing it from every angle.

Now Cassian's eyes opened and he raised his head, an expression of fierce determination on his noble features.

'Thank you, Emperor, for your guidance,' he intoned. 'Thank you, primarch, for your clarity. I will not fail you again.'

Cassian rose and sheathed his blade. He flexed his wounded arm experimentally, nodding to himself as he felt reknitted muscle tense and reset bone hold strong.

'Sufficient,' he said. 'There is much to be done.'

An hour later, Cassian held his council of war within the lower narthex of the cathedrum. Rainwater dripped through shattered windows and fell from ragged holes in the ceiling high above. A foul mist drifted at ankle height, while plump flies meandered through the still air. Stained glass crunched underfoot as Cassian, Keritraeus, Dematris and their senior sergeants gathered. The two Dreadnought battle-brothers were also present, for they had fought since the earliest days of the Indomitus Crusade and had gained much strategic insight. The Cadian captain Dzansk completed the gathering, albeit as a grainy green ghost beamed from a holoprojector.

'Honoured warriors of the Imperium,' began Cassian, 'we have suffered at the hands of the heretic invaders, but that ends now. We are going to defeat them in the Emperor's name, and see to it that every trace of their filth is cleansed from this world.'

Several of his sergeants slammed their fists against their chest-plates in salute, and Brother Marius rumbled a near-subsonic 'Hear, hear.'

'We are with you, lieutenant,' said Keritraeus. 'But how?'

'The Emperor has gifted me with insight into the minds of our foes,' said Cassian. 'They worship a god of plagues, and are empowered by his unclean gifts. I believe that their god, and by extension the Death Guard themselves, derive much of their power from sickness and misery – from entropy.'

'Based on what, brother?' asked Dematris.

'Consider,' said Cassian. 'They bombarded the city before their initial landing. Why use a mixture of targeted ordnance and bio-phages? Why not just hammer Dustrious into ruin and move on? With so superior a force, it was strategically inefficient at best.'

'The astropathic fortress, brother-lieutenant,' said Sergeant Gallen. 'I would suggest that they want to capture the astropaths and use them for their own purposes.'

'Likely, but then, they have overwhelming numbers – if they had wished to crush Imperial resistance here and claim their prize, they could have done so in a matter of hours, not weeks. I mean no disrespect to your brave fighting men and women, Captain Dzansk.'

'*No offence taken, my lord,*' said Dzansk in a static-furred voice. '*We have been wondering the same thing since day one. It seems unlikely that the enemy commander is so incompetent as to have misjudged the comparative disposition of our forces. Our best guess was that he was waiting for something, perhaps for sickness to decimate our ranks.*'

'In a way, I believe that he was,' said Cassian. 'I believe our enemy is deliberately drawing this battle out. The Death Guard are causing as much misery and suffering as they possibly can, for by doing so they best honour their god.'

'A devotional offering,' said Dematris in disgust. 'They torment this planet and its populace as one might light candles in an Imperial shrine.'

'I fear that, if you are correct, it may be worse still,' said Keritraeus. 'I told you that the empyrean feels agitated here.'

'You did,' said Cassian, 'but is that not simply the aftermath of the warp storm that marooned us?'

'I thought so at first,' said Keritraeus, 'but if you are right about this, then the storm on high, the agitation in the warp, the silence of the astropaths... It could be the effects of a wider, ongoing ritual – signs that the Death Guard are making an offering to their god, and that it is being accepted.'

'You're talking about the summoning of daemons,' said Dematris.

'Perhaps,' said Keritraeus, 'or some other foulness that sane minds cannot even guess at. Whatever the case, it seems logical that the astropaths would be the final offering, the heart's blood that seals the compact.'

'By the Throne!' said Aggressor Sergeant Temeter. 'If this is true then the heretics are using this entire world as their sacrificial altar. The consequences of such a vast ritual would surely be disastrous.'

'Just so,' said Cassian. 'You see now why we cannot continue to offer this enemy a battle of attrition. That is precisely the war they want. We must resolve this swiftly and decisively, and capture the astropathic fortress before they are able to make use of it.'

'I ask again,' said Keritraeus. 'How? Impetuosity has already failed us once. They outnumber us, even with the Cadians added to our own forces. Our losses during the ambush were considerable, and even with the *Primarch's Sword* to support us, I believe we will be hard-pressed to defeat this foe.'

'In a straight fight, that is true,' agreed Cassian, 'but just as they are the twisted progeny of their primarch, so we are the true sons of ours. We will outmanoeuvre them, find their weaknesses and exploit them. Their heretical faith compels them to behave in ways that seem like madness. They may be working to a plan that we cannot fully fathom, but they have also ignored strategic practicals that we will not.'

Cassian felt a frisson of disquiet at how closely his

own words echoed those of the farseer, but he pressed on regardless.

'Sergeant Marcus has identified one such strategic option,' he said, turning to the Reiver sergeant.

Marcus nodded. 'During our scouting sweep, we located a partial tunnel entrance at this location,' he said, exloading coordinates to his comrades' auspex-maps. 'It lies amidst the ruins of a generatorum block, and presumably was opened by the enemy's initial bombardment. Binaric interrogation of functioning cogitators within the generatorum complex revealed this as an entrance to Dustrious' municipalis support grid. It's a backup power supply, whose conduits run beneath the astropathic fortress.'

'Is it a route in, then?' asked Keritraeus. 'If so, are we to assume that the enemy have simply overlooked it by chance?'

'To the first question, yes, we believe so,' replied Marcus. 'Data-schematics suggest that an exit hatch could be used to emerge within the outer cloisters of the fortress. But to the second, no, the enemy have not overlooked it.'

'How can you be sure?'

'We eliminated a small herd of the plague mutants penned in a cordon around the entrance. We further disarmed a substantial quantity of tripwires linked to viral grenades, and heard the groans of more of the creatures from the tunnel's mouth. They were not there by chance.'

'Then we are to believe they have simply ignored this route into the heart of the fortress?' asked Dematris doubtfully.

'The tunnel confines would be tight,' said Marcus. 'An unaugmented human could progress down them, or Primaris Marines in light combat armour such as my Reiver squad. Anyone larger would struggle. The exit point would also be overlooked by servitor-guns on both the outer and inner fortifications. Attrition amongst the initial attackers would be high.'

'All of which, the Death Guard could have overcome with sufficient ingenuity and belligerence,' said Cassian. 'But I believe that doing so would have ended their war too soon. A virus that kills its host is inefficient, and ultimately self-destructive. To thrive, it must allow its victim to live.'

'At least for as long as serves its needs,' added Keritraeus, nodding. 'So how do we exploit this omission by our foes? We can hardly move the bulk of our forces through such a narrow conduit.'

'True,' said Cassian, 'but we can send Squad Marcus through it, and thus gain access to the fortress. The Reivers will link up with whatever garrison remains within. They will manually direct its guns, and stand ready to support our strike for the gates.'

'It's to be another direct assault, then?' asked Dematris.

'A coordinated strike,' replied Cassian, 'with the intent of denying the enemy their prize and contacting the crusade's forces. We cannot overcome this foe with our current strength, but nor can we leave them to complete whatever foul ritual they are attempting. Thus, if we cannot rejoin the crusade as duty compels, we will bring the crusade to us.'

His comrades nodded. He saw hope in their eyes.

'Captain Dzansk,' said Cassian. 'Are you ready to serve your Emperor?'

'Always, my lord. Cadia stands.'

'Very well. What I ask of you is no easy thing, captain, but it must be thus. You will mobilise all your remaining forces and engage the Death Guard in a diversionary attack shortly before we launch our own assault. Draw them in, and tie up as much of their strength as you can.'

'That will cost us dear, my lord,' said Dzansk. *'Many of my soldiers are sick, or wounded. Our ammunition stocks are low. If the Death Guard respond in force, we will not endure their wrath for long.'*

'I understand,' said Cassian. 'While your forces engage the enemy, ours will move swiftly into position and secure the main fortress gate. Sergeant Marcus will already be inside, and he will open it to allow us access. We will then hold the gate for you for as long as we can before falling back within.'

'Yes, my lord.'

Cassian heard something in the captain's voice – doubt, perhaps – but victory here was too important. So long as the Cadians did their part in the Emperor's name, that was what truly mattered.

'Keritraeus,' he said, 'what of the enemy's apparent invisibility to our auspex?'

'The storm continues to interfere,' replied the Librarian. 'And in theory, they may be able to conceal themselves as they did before their ambush. But we have visual confirmation from our Inceptor squads as to enemy movements. After the ambush, the Death Guard appear to have tightened their cordon around the astropathic fortress.'

Cassian nodded, then addressed Dzansk's hologram again.

'Captain Dzansk, ready your forces to launch their attack at seventeen hundred hours sidereal. Sergeant Marcus, you know your duty?'

'I do, brother-lieutenant,' said Marcus with a salute.

'Then ready yourselves, brothers. We go into battle again, and this time to victory or death.'

Lord Gurloch stood amidst the ruins of the Mons Aquilas counting house and stared up the hill at the astropathic fortress. Another wave of groaning pox-walkers was stumbling towards it, falling rank by rank to the fortress' guns.

'How soon… until the loyalists attack… again?' asked Thrax.

Gurloch responded with a heavy shrug that sent foul fluids trickling down his armour.

'We gave them a sound beating, for all that they wounded us also, but the Emperor's lapdogs have never known when to admit defeat. I doubt they'll be dissuaded for long.'

'Should we… accelerate… the attack?'

'And spoil so fine a broth?' asked Gurloch in a tone of genuine surprise. 'No, Thrax. Allowing these new arrivals to force our hand would waste all our hard work. The sorcerers assure me the empyrean churns like a cauldron of poxes. Beyond the veil, our plague of misery is brewing nicely. Let the loyalists come at us again, and again. We have the numbers, the commanding ground, and the gifts of Nurgle and Mortarion both. We are Death Guard, Thrax – we will endure while they suffer and die.'

'And when… the plague is… ready?' asked the Biologis Putrifier.

Gurloch heard the relish in his gargling voice, and knew that Thrax already knew the answer to his question; he just liked to hear it spoken aloud.

'Why then, old friend, we will demonstrate the true generosity of Nurgle,' he said. 'We will swat aside the paltry forces arrayed against us, claim the astropathic fortress for our own and use its psycho-amplific machineries as the vector for our wondrous new disease. We will disperse it through the ether like flies from a bursting corpse, like spores from fungus, like Nurgle's Rot through a healthy body. We will beam our psychic contagion across the stars to every Imperial world in this sector. We will raise an epidemic the like of which has not been seen in millennia.'

'And with it… we will praise… Nurgle.'

'And with it,' said Gurloch cheerily, 'we will earn Nurgle's praise!'

CHAPTER SEVEN

Dropping down into the ferrocrete confines of the tunnel, Reiver Sergeant Marcus held his bolt carbine in one hand and his long blade in the other. His auto-senses overlaid his sight with multiple spectra, driving back the darkness and revealing shambling half-shapes amidst the deeper shadows.

As expected, bulky power conduits took up most of the tunnel space, while the ceiling was low enough that Marcus was forced to stoop to avoid catching his skull-faced helm on low pipes and jutting gauge assemblies.

'Targets ahead,' he voxed to his squad. 'We're going to have to advance single file and engage as best we can. Brother Ignatio, you have rearguard. Brother Tanus, mapping. Keep us on the right path if we're busy with battle. Blades only unless in extremis.'

Vox clicks came back to him, signals that his squad

ANDY CLARK

had received and understood their orders. There were eight of them in all, down from ten after the hard-fought battle earlier that day – more than enough, however, to complete their mission.

Sergeant Marcus led off along the tunnel, setting a swift pace. The first plague mutant died before it even knew he was there, his blade punching through the back of its neck and all but sawing its head off. The second fell as it turned towards him, a foot-and-a-half of combat knife sliding through its eye socket into its rotted brain.

More of the creatures staggered towards him, their moans filling the enclosed space. The sounds made him feel nauseous, as though some sort of poison were seeping into his mind.

'Mute your audio-intakes,' he ordered as he hacked and tore his way through the creatures. 'Vox communication only.'

'You feel that too, sergeant?' asked Tanus.

'There is some heretical taint to their voices. I will not risk its corruption.' Marcus punched his gun butt into another rotting face, shattering the thing's blast goggles and snapping its head back in a spray of fluids. The corpse-mutant crumpled, still grinning. 'That's the last of them for now.'

'Movement at our rear, sergeant,' said Brother Ignatio.

'Keep moving,' he replied. 'We can't let these abominations slow us down, or the whole attack fails.'

He set off along the tunnel, scanning the darkness for threats and watching the chronometer on his helm display as it ticked slowly downwards.

* * *

Captain Dzansk stood atop a Chimera, ignoring the oily rain that poured down upon him. He surveyed the last of his forces, a few hundred fighting men and women clad in the battered and stained uniforms of the Cadian Imperial Guard. The last few regimental preachers and commissars moved through the ranks, offering a muttered benediction here, a stern gaze there. A half-company of Leman Russ tanks idled off to one side, engines rumbling while their commanders sat high in their cupolas to listen to his address.

'Soldiers of Cadia!' began Dzansk, his voice amplified through the speaker on Voxman Kavier's pack. 'You have fought long and hard for this world, and I salute your tenacity! Your bravery! Your faith!'

Many of his warriors made the sign of the aquila, but their faces remained grim. They knew what was coming.

'Yet our work is not done,' said Dzansk. 'The enemy remains. Our Emperor asks more of us, and we shall answer, "Yes!"'

He saw the determination in their faces. They were strong, Cadian steel still in their spines despite the weeks of hardship they had endured and the threat of almost-certain death.

'The heretic foe have poured their filth down upon us. They have inflicted every hardship and horror that they could. Lesser soldiers would have faltered long ago, but still we stand strong! I look upon you and see not broken souls, but brave soldiers of the Imperium, and it swells my heart with pride!'

He saw a few heads rise a little at that, a few shoulders straighten.

'Perhaps our enemy thought us defeated, just as the Despoiler thought us defeated when he shattered our world beneath our feet! But we were not defeated then, and we are not defeated now! I keep Kasr Partox in my heart, and I know you all do too! Today we go into battle alongside the glorious Adeptus Astartes of the Ultramarines Chapter, in the service of no less than Primarch Roboute Guilliman himself, and we will prevail!'

This raised a cheer at last, albeit a hollow one. He saw the waxy pallor of his soldiers' skin, the lesions and marks of sickness that clung to so many, just as they marred his own flesh beneath his sodden uniform. Dzansk and his regiment had been immersed for too long amidst the contagions of the enemy – and put down too many of their own sick – to believe that they were making it off Kalides alive. He had agreed when Lieutenant Cassian had outlined his plan to retreat through the gates of the astropathic fortress, but he had done so knowing that he could not risk bringing disease inside those walls.

'Be strong, brothers and sisters of Cadia!' he cried. 'Gird your hearts with faith. Armour your souls with contempt. And remember that to die in the Emperor's name is an honour without compare!'

He clambered down from his perch and boarded his transport, Kavier and the drafted replacements for his command squad following him in.

'Soldiers of Cadia,' voxed Dzansk as he strapped himself into his restraints. 'In the Emperor's name – advance.'

* * *

'It is all of them, lord,' said Blorthos. 'I can see them moving like maggots through the corpse of this city.'

Gurloch led the Witherlings down a half-flooded processional, Plague Marines and thrumming bloat-drones following in his wake. He shook his head in disgust at Blorthos' words.

'Such a waste,' he said. 'These fools had days and days of sickness and sorrow yet to offer up. Now the Ultramarines throw their allies' lives away, and for what? A distraction.'

'They are… ignorant creatures… lord,' came Thrax's voice over the vox.

'So be it,' sighed Gurloch heavily. 'These Imperials have no idea how to savour their own suffering. Once again, they prove themselves ungrateful. My patience with them has run out.'

'The… Space Marines…' Thrax began, but Gurloch cut him off, suddenly irked by his subordinate's gasping voice.

'The Space Marines will undoubtedly strike when they believe us sufficiently engaged. Perhaps they will even bombard us from orbit again. None of that matters. They clearly want the astropathic fortress as much as we do, so let's give them a little false hope.'

'Lord?'

'Send in another wave of poxwalkers,' said Gurloch. 'A big one. Enough to keep the guns busy for a spell. Use them as cover and pull back to within the shadow of the fortress walls, then dig in. The Ultramarines won't risk dropping barrage bombs and lance strikes so close to their objective, so they'll have to dislodge you the old-fashioned way.'

'They can... try,' said Thrax scornfully.

'Exactly. Hold them there for me, Thrax. I will finish the Astra Militarum and then return, and between us we will hurl back the surviving Ultramarines a second time. Such a bitter mix of disappointment and suffering will surely be enough to perfect our plague.'

'In Mortarion's name... it will... be done.'

'Eighth Platoon,' voxed Dzansk. 'Move up through those ruins and secure firing positions. Signal when you're in place, then cover Fifth as they attack.'

Voices came back to him over the rattle and thump of gunfire, tight acknowledgements of orders received. The Cadians had advanced to within two miles of the fortress before meeting resistance amidst a district of old, rusting chem factories. Now they were fighting to gain ground, Dzansk still pushing his soldiers forward as aggressively as he dared.

'Captain, Third Platoon reports more Death Guard moving north of their position,' said Kavier. 'Heavy infantry and several tanks, Predator-class.'

'They'll be outflanked,' said Gunner Astin, tightening her grip on Chonsky's old meltagun.

'Gatekeeper, do you read?' voxed Dzansk. 'Sergeant Yuri?'

'Affirmative, captain,' came Yuri's voice, lousy with static. 'Awaiting orders.'

'Third are about to be outflanked to the north,' said Dzansk. 'Intercede. Take Kasr's Fury with you.'

'Understood,' said Yuri. 'We'll hammer those heretics all the way back to the warp.'

'Good man,' said Dzansk. He knew that two Leman

Russ tanks wouldn't be enough to overcome the enemy force that Third Platoon had reported. Sergeant Yuri probably knew it too.

At this stage, it was something of a moot point.

'This is Sergeant Chenska, Second Platoon,' came a desperate voice over the vox. *'We're overrun. They're pushing up through–'* The voice cut out, replaced by the scream of lasgun fire. Something exploded with a dull thump, before the voice returned. *'Repeat, Second Platoon is overrun. Enemy infantry and Dreadnought-class walkers are pushing up through refinery one-nine.'*

'Understood, Chenska,' said Dzansk. 'Can you extract?'

'Negative, command, negative,' said Chenska as gunfire blared again. *'They've pushed past us. We're holed up in the administratum wing but we don't have long. I'm ordering all grenades primed. We'll bring the roof down on these heretic bastards.'*

'Go with the Emperor's grace, sergeant,' said Dzansk.

'Cadia stands! Cadia st–'

Static swallowed her voice.

Dzansk balled one fist and thumped it against the Chimera's bulkhead, hard enough to hurt.

'Captain,' said Kavier, 'Eighth report heavy drone presence on the ridge. They've been driven back. *Martyr's Fist* and *Imperius* have moved to support. Sir, Commissar Durent has taken command of Fifth Platoon – they're attacking despite the lack of covering fire. Taking massive casualties.'

'Of course they are,' said Dzansk. For a moment, he felt nothing but an incredible weight of exhaustion. Yet anger at his own weakness eclipsed it, and faith burned hot in its wake. 'Lieutenant Cassian,' he voxed, switching channels.

'Captain,' came the Ultramarine's voice.

'I estimate that we have minutes at best, my lord,' said Dzansk. 'I can't listen to my soldiers die without me any longer. I'm joining the fight.'

'No word yet from Squad Marcus,' replied Cassian. *'We are moving up on the hab-district south of the fortress now. Encountering increasing Death Guard resistance. I need you to give us as long as you possibly can, captain.'*

'With respect, my lord, I've been fifteen years in the Guard. I fought at Kasr Sonnen. I fought on Thracian Primaris. I fought on the Partox Fields when the Despoiler came for my world. I've fought on half a dozen planets since, and I have never, ever given less than my all for the Emperor. The same is true of every single soldier I lead into battle, so you can be damn well assured that we don't need your urging to fight this fight to our last breath.'

'Very good, captain,' said Cassian. *'We are fighting too close to the fortress walls to risk deployment of orbital ordnance. Shall I re-task Shipmaster Aethor to support your efforts?'*

'Yes, my lord,' said Dzansk. 'Let cleansing fire rain down upon them.'

'Go with the Emperor's blessings, Captain Dzansk. It has been an honour.'

'And you, Lieutenant Cassian. Make this count.'

Dzansk cut the feed, checked that his laspistol was charged and his grenade belt clipped in place, and then thumbed the tank's internal intercom. 'Driver, take us in. Let's give these faithless traitors a taste of Cadian steel.'

'Absolutely, sir,' came the reply, and with a roar the Chimera surged forwards.

'Get that top hatch open,' said Dzansk. 'Gunners, grant the Emperor's mercy to anything that moves.'

'Yes, sir!' chorused Astin and Nils, releasing the locking bolts on the Chimera's roof hatch. They heaved the doors open with a clang and hauled themselves up into firing positions. Dzansk joined them, laspistol in hand, while Kavier added his own lasgun to the arsenal. Behind them, Colour Sergeant Bastel unfurled the banner and raised it high, allowing it to stream out behind the Chimera as it sped between the crumbling ruins.

Lasfire flashed in the chem factory to Dzansk's right, and the clouds glowed as the first orbital lance beams stabbed down into the battle. Through the driving rain, Dzansk saw bulky shapes loom at the intersection ahead. Bolt shells started to clang from the Chimera's hull and whip past his head.

The Chimera's turret tracked and fired, its multi-laser spitting shots into the enemy. The heavy bolter in the hull joined in, thumping shells back at the traitors.

'Pick your targets,' ordered Dzansk. 'Fire at will!'

As the Chimera ploughed through the intersection, Plague Marines scattered before it. Dzansk fired his laspistol, shots scorching the heretics' armour. Gunner Astin's meltagun gave its breathy roar, and Nils' plasma gun joined in with a deafening scream. Their fire turned one heretic to glowing ash and took the legs off another. Lasfire from Dzansk, Kavier and Bastel blew a third Plague Marine from his feet, then their tank was across the intersection and racing away down the street.

'Excellent marksmanship,' said Dzansk, grinning fiercely despite himself. 'Driver, circle through those ruins towards the Eighth. We'll lend them our support.'

Overhead the sky caught fire again as a lance strike speared downwards and detonated a chem factory. The entire structure collapsed, no doubt burying Cadians and heretics alike. The Chimera slewed around a rain-slick corner, then Dzansk had to cling on tightly as the armoured transport swerved sharply, narrowly missing the burning wreck of a Leman Russ sat in the middle of the street.

Dzansk saw the words *Martyr's Fist* still legible on the wreck's bubbling paintwork.

'Enemies ahead,' voxed the driver. 'Captain, get back inside! Now!'

Dzansk glimpsed a nightmarish mechanical contraption squatting amidst the ruins in front of them, Cadian corpses heaped around it. He had an impression of an armoured mass covered in spikes and guns, with armoured arachnoid limbs and a ghoulish death mask. The cannon that jutted from the monstrosity's chest fired, and a sudden hammer blow knocked the breath from Dzansk's lungs.

Suddenly he was tumbling through the air, rain and fire and hurtling ferrocrete all around him. Something hit his cheek, and pain exploded through his jaw. Something else detonated in a cloud of flames and whizzing metal.

Then Dzansk hit the roadway with tremendous force and blacked out.

* * *

...Gunner Astin, blood running down her cheek, a chunk of metal piercing her torso, still bracing and firing her meltagun with a scream of defiance. Blood bursting from her as her body jerks and dances...

...boots thumping near his head, jolting him from darkness, running past him. Screams. Gunfire...

...a familiar figure crawling towards him. Something bulky on its back. Fire. Fire dancing down its limbs, in its hair. Kavier, reaching out towards him, then slumping face first in the rain...

...darkness and grey...

...water and flame...

Dzansk groaned and rolled onto his back, then gasped in pain as the motion caused his broken bones to grind together. He opened his eyes, vision swimming, and felt agony radiating from every part of him.

Kavier!

He looked, and saw Kavier's burned corpse sprawled in the roadway, a dozen yards from a crater full of mangled metal that used to be a Chimera.

Dzansk groaned again, reaching a tentative hand up then snatching it away as he felt how horribly mangled his jaw was; his hand came away soaked in blood.

Running on nothing but defiance, Dzansk forced himself to his feet. His right arm hung uselessly by his side, white bone showing through a rip in the blood-drenched cloth of his sleeve. More blood ran freely from cuts and contusions all over his body, and Dzansk was glad that he couldn't see what he looked like at that moment.

A corpse too stubborn to die, he thought, then

recoiled at the mental image of the enemy's plague mutants.

Through a haze of pain, he grasped that he was alone. Kavier, Astin and Bastel lay dead in the street. Nils was nowhere to be seen. The monstrous spider-engine was gone too, no doubt stalking away to slaughter the last of his regiment.

Captain Dzansk stood alone, mortally wounded, drenched with rain and full of sorrow and hate. He limped down the street and bent over Bastel's mangled body. With his one good arm, he fumbled at the pole of the regimental standard. It took him three attempts, but he managed to hoist the rain-slick pole aloft. The banner still hung from it, singed and stained but in one piece.

Dzansk turned from the wreck and began to limp, one step at a time, towards the distant sound of gunfire. While there was breath in his body, he thought, he would continue to do what he could.

Heavy footsteps behind Dzansk made him turn, and he leaned on the banner pole for support. His eyes widened as he saw hulking Terminators lumbering towards him. At their head strode a horn-helmed monster with a tri-bladed axe.

The enemy's leader, he thought feverishly. It had to be.

He cast about himself for a weapon, or for a vox headset to call down fire on his own position. *Anything.*

The huge Chaos lord lumbered closer, engulfing Dzansk in a sweat-thick reek of putrefaction that made him gag, then groan at the agony that that motion caused him. Hate flared in his chest as he realised the figure was laughing.

'By Grandfather's cauldron!' exclaimed the Terminator. His voice was a deep, bubbling horror, like the last death rattle of a dozen drowning men. 'This must be the leader of this merry band of fools.'

Dzansk tried to limp backwards, still casting desperately around for a gun. If he could reach Astin's body, then perhaps Chonsky's meltagun could strike one more blow before the end. That spark of hope fizzled out as the hulking Terminators surrounded him, hemming him inside a ring of rusted, seeping metal and flyblown flesh. The stench was almost more than he could bear.

Dzansk leaned on the banner pole and hauled himself upright, staring defiantly as the horn-helmed lord loomed over him.

'You stand in the presence of Lord Gurloch,' snarled one of the Terminators, a disgusting vision with a single bulbous eye where his head should be. 'You should be on your knees, worm.'

'No, Blorthos,' said Gurloch. 'No, this one has earned the right to stand.' He looked down upon Dzansk, whose hate-filled stare didn't waver. 'Look at you. Jaw hanging by sinews. Arm broken. Organs ruptured, bones cracked, flesh veritably seething with disease. And still you refuse to fall. In another life, my father might have welcomed you with open arms.'

Dzansk tried to speak, but managed nothing more than a slurry of bloodied grunts. Lord Gurloch laughed again, his mirth as genuine as it was horrifying.

'I shall assume that whatever you were attempting to say, it was somewhat less complimentary,' he said, eliciting cruel chuckles from his warriors. Off in the distance, something exploded as lance fire stabbed down from the sky.

'You have proven yourself a stubborn and tenacious foe,' said Gurloch, his tone growing serious, 'and for that I salute you. But your mind is closed, your eyes shut to the glory of Chaos, and you have cost me time and warriors.'

He reached out and grasped the banner pole, plucking it from Dzansk's hands as easily as taking a toy from a child. Gurloch cast the banner into the mud, then wrapped his fingers around Dzansk's neck and hoisted him easily off the ground.

The captain gurgled in agony as broken bones crunched together in his jaw, Gurloch's rust-metal fingers tightening on his windpipe and vertebrae. His good arm twitched and spasmed as he felt rot spreading through his flesh from the heretic's touch.

'I am done with your little soldiers,' said Gurloch. 'I have wrung the last droplets of misery and pain from your husks. Now you will die, then the Ultramarines will die, and then – at *last* – I will be free to spread the blessings of Nurgle across the stars.'

Dzansk was dying, his tormentor's words echoing to him down a long, dark tunnel. His fingers twitched with the last flickers of his life. He felt them touch something.

Cold metal.

Pin.

In his pain and bewilderment, he had forgotten. But now he remembered, and he wordlessly thanked the Emperor for this final gift.

With his last breath, Captain Dzansk summoned the

strength to pluck out the pin and let it tumble slowly away. He went with it, drifting into darkness like an autumn leaf on the Partox fields of home.

He was already dead when the krak grenades on his belt exploded.

CHAPTER EIGHT

Cassian charged up a heap of rain-slick rubble, shrugging bolt-rounds from his shoulder guard. He swept Duty in a killing arc, lopping off the end of the Plague Marine's gun along with the fleshy tentacle that held it.

His enemy bellowed in anger and tried to smash his mailed fist into Cassian's faceplate. The lieutenant wove aside and slashed his sword through his enemy's legs, causing the heretic to fall to his knees. Cassian pressed his bolt rifle one-handed against his enemy's helm and blew off his head.

'They're retreating to the next line,' voxed Dematris. 'Heavy covering fire coming down from the right. Brother-lieutenant, they're digging in again.'

A spray of diseased filth rained down from above, and Cassian threw himself out of its path. He cursed as droplets spattered his armour, causing ceramite to hiss and bubble. The remaining two battle-brothers of Intercessor squad Telor were less fortunate: they staggered in pain as their armoured forms were eaten away by virulent bacteria.

'Brothers, find cover and suppress the enemy,' ordered Cassian. 'Inceptors, encircle their position to the right and open the way for Aggressor squad Doras to turn their flank.'

The Ultramarines were less than half a mile from the front gate of the astropathic fortress, but Cassian felt his frustration growing with every second. The enemy had dug in with veteran skill. Every time the Ultramarines overran one Death Guard position, they found themselves enfiladed from two more. They were pressing forwards through the rubble heaps and ruins of the hab-district, but not quickly enough. Close by, Cassian could hear the endless groans of plague mutants and the chatter of the fortress' wall guns.

Again, he tried to raise anyone within the fortress by vox. Again, he met with silence. He switched channels, attempting to contact Captain Dzansk.

He heard nothing but static.

'Keritraeus,' he voxed. 'Are you in position?'

'Almost, lieutenant,' came the Librarian's reply. *'They mined the transitway and packed the buildings with Plague Marines.* Pride of Talassar *took some damage pushing around their flank, but the combined fire of the Repulsors and the Dreadnoughts is too much for them. They are falling back, and we will be in position in less than a minute.'*

'Make it sooner. If we haven't heard from Sergeant Marcus by then, we–'

Cassian was interrupted by a flashing priority rune

in his peripheral vision. He blink-clicked it, and felt relief as he heard Sergeant Marcus' voice.

'*Lieutenant, this is Marcus, do you read?*'

'Go ahead, sergeant,' said Cassian.

'*We were delayed, brother-lieutenant. We had to cut through a bulkhead that wasn't on the maps. Then, upon emerging into the cloisters, we came under heavy fire.*'

'Fire?' exclaimed Cassian. 'Have the enemy gained the fortress already?'

'*Negative,*' said Marcus. '*Lieutenant, everyone's dead. The fortress… Some sort of plague has spread here. The garrison have been rotting for days.*'

'Then the gunfire…?'

'*Automated servitor protocols. I lost Brother Archimaeus to them before we were able to reach the overseer shrine and repurpose the guns.*'

'Primarch's blood,' cursed Cassian. 'If plague has spread within the walls, then the astropathic choir is no more. We can't contact the crusade.'

'*No sign of any dead astropaths yet, my lord. And we've only seen part of the outer cloisters – it is possible that there are survivors deeper within, quarantined against the contagions.*'

'*Do we proceed?*' asked Keritraeus. '*I'm in position, but I can't hold here long.*'

'We proceed,' said Cassian. 'There is still hope. The Emperor would not abandon us so. Besides, if all else fails, we can use the fortress as a strongpoint while we plan our next move.'

And, whispered a traitorous thought in his mind, *she said you would live to fight for Yme'Loc…*

The voice of Chaplain Dematris came over the vox,

addressing the entire strike force. *'With zeal and determination, we shall overcome the works of these heretics,'* he bellowed. *'Believe in your primarch and the Emperor! Make their strength yours! Strike now for Macragge and the Golden Throne!'*

Keritraeus stormed out from cover with his force staff held high. His eyes flashed with power as he summoned the might of the empyrean, then unleashed it in a searing column of flame. The psychic blast leapt up the flank of the rubble mound and detonated at its peak. Blazing Plague Marines tumbled from behind improvised barricades; he snatched one up with the power of his mind, crushing the heretic's armour before hurling his mangled body at two of his blazing comrades.

To the Librarian's right, the two Repulsor tanks thundered forwards on pummelling cushions of grav-energy. They swept up the rubble, pounding it flat as they unleashed hails of bolts, shells and las-blasts. The Plague Marines guarding the enemy's left flank fired back, but several of their number burst messily under the Repulsors' combined fire, while others were left reeling as limbs were blown off and torsos torn open.

To Keritraeus' left, the strike force's two Redemptor Dreadnoughts advanced, servo-motors whining and generators roaring as they climbed the rubble slope. Brother Marius' onslaught cannon screamed as it spat streams of fire into the Death Guard, while Brother Indomator's macro plasma incinerator glowed and vented steam as it fired again and again.

'Forward!' ordered Keritraeus, gathering warp energies and using them to leap high into the air and sweep down atop the traitors' blazing position. 'Do not relent!'

Death Guard lumbered along the top of the rubble ridge, bringing their guns to bear against the Ultramarines' flanking force. Blight-ridden projectiles rained down, chewing a blackened crater in Brother Marius' sarcophagus and stripping the las-talon from *Maximus' Revenge*.

A sudden storm of bolt rifle fire engulfed the traitors as, several hundred yards away, Cassian pushed his squads up in the centre. In their urgency to halt the flank attack, the Plague Marines had allowed themselves to be silhouetted atop the ridge. The Intercessors made them pay for their error, bolt shells and grenades blasting filthy chunks from the Death Guard. Some of the traitors fell dead. Others stubbornly fired back.

'Be advised,' came Sergeant Marcus' voice over the vox. *'The plague mutant numbers between you and the walls are thinning. We are repurposing half the wall guns to target the Death Guard.'*

Keritraeus reached for the energies of the warp again, but snatched his mind back as he felt dark power surging beyond the veil. The warding circuits in his psychic hood glowed, and he let out a relieved breath as the danger passed. Conjuring psychic powers was dangerous at the best of times, risking the attention of hungry warp entities that sought to possess or consume mortal minds; now, with the empyrean churning with amassed ritual energies, it was hazardous in the extreme.

Still, he stopped for a moment, brow creased as he reached tentatively out with his mind.

'Something…' he muttered, questing with his senses. There.

Keritraeus keyed his vox.

'Cassian,' he said. 'The warp grows wrathful.'

'More so?' asked Cassian.

'More so,' echoed Keritraeus. 'I sense malefic entities gathering to the slaughter. Whether this is what the heretics intended or no, it bodes ill for us if these warp predators pierce the veil.'

'Understood. Their line is about to break.'

Ahead, Keritraeus saw the Aggressors of Squad Doras crest the other flank of the rubble rise. Their boltstorm gauntlets roared, spitting out a hail of fire that drove the Death Guard back and sent several of their number crashing to the ground.

Figures moved amidst a ruin at the centre of the Death Guard line. Keritraeus saw the glint of light on tainted glass and drew breath to shout a warning.

Too late.

A hail of bulbous spheres sailed through the air, blight grenades plucked from the bone spines of a Death Guard alchemist and hurled by his comrades. The spheres smashed down upon Squad Doras, drenching the Aggressors in diseased slime. The Ultramarines roared in pain and shock as their flesh blistered and rotted, foul buboes rising and bursting across their bodies even as their armour rusted and corroded.

One by one, Squad Doras staggered and fell.

Aghast, Keritraeus summoned a surge of energy with

which to exact revenge, but the traitors were already gone, using the Ultramarines' moment of horrified distraction to fall back.

'The way is open,' voxed Lieutenant Cassian. 'But at a price. For our fallen battle-brothers, advance.'

Lord Gurloch stomped through the rain, his grip flexing and tightening upon the haft of his plaguereaper. His good cheer had evaporated, leaving a scummy film of anger in its wake. The Cadians had delayed him far longer than he had expected, and injured him sorely. His chest was rent and mangled, and the faceplate of his helm had cracked to reveal part of his pox-raddled face and one yellowed eye. The wounds done to his body by the Cadian captain's grenades were closing as his flesh gouted layers of pus and blubber, but he could feel the ache of shrapnel still buried deep within him.

Blorthos was dead, and two of his Witherlings wounded beyond the abilities of their god-given gifts to heal. The Terminator champion had foreseen the danger at the last second, wrenching the Cadian from Gurloch's grip just as the detonations triggered. Gurloch intended to ensure that the loyalists paid dearly for his death.

'Lord…' came Thrax's voice over the vox. 'Our position… is overrun. They have… retrained the fortress' guns.'

Gurloch's foul mood darkened further.

'Rot them all,' he snarled. 'Have they contacted the garrison? Do people still live within the fortress?'

'Unclear…'

'Thrax, do not let them through the fortress gates.

Wringing misery and suffering from a human garrison before striking the killing blow, that is one thing. But attempting to overthrow such a fastness when Space Marines hold the walls? No – they may be weak loyalists, but even so they could sterilise the entire ritual.'

'We may… not be able…to stop them… They have… numbers… momentum… Our casualties are heavy and our position… poor.'

Gurloch stared through the rain towards the fortress, still a mile ahead. He looked around at the trudging advance of his warriors, relentless but far from swift. A handful of daemonically powered bloat-drones thrummed along in their midst, their rusted turbines droning like giant flies' wings.

'The drones could reach you in time,' he said.

'I doubt… they would be enough,' replied Thrax, breaking off for a moment as gunfire roared and explosions thundered. 'I am sorry… lord.'

'Save your apologies – they'll sicken no one. Just make their advance as costly as you can, Thrax. I will do the rest.'

Gurloch cut the vox-link, switching channels to address the trio of Death Guard sorcerers that served his forces. He disliked the muttering plaguecasters intensely, a trait he had inherited from Primarch Mortarion himself. He dealt with the plague witches only when he had to.

Now was such a time.

'Noxgol, Shunngh, Scrofule,' he said. 'Heed the words of your lord.'

A chorus of replies came back to him: one voice

droning, another wheezing, another sing-song and completely insane.

'The suffering of this world has been magnificent,' said Gurloch. 'Much misery has gathered beyond the veil for our grand purpose. But if we wish to secure victory, then a little of Nurgle's beneficence must be vomited forth.'

'*You wish us to open the Garden gates, my lord?*' asked Scrofule.

'A mere crack – sufficient just to bog the enemy down and stop them from gaining sanctuary within the fortress.'

'*You ask much, lord,*' said Shunngh breathlessly. '*The daemons of great Nurgle are no mere foot soldiers, for you to command at will. Once the way is open, they may force it wider. It could mean our souls to deny them.*'

'There are three of you,' replied Gurloch scornfully. 'A tri-lobe. Surely enough to do as I ask. Open the way, and retain control. I care not what it costs you, but understand this – if you throw the floodgates wide and waste the great bounty we have harvested here, then whatever torments you can imagine, I will show you far worse.'

His sorcerers chorused their assent, and Gurloch dismissed them with a thought. Ahead he could hear the clangour of battle, growing closer by the moment. Overhead the clouds roiled and churned like a dying man's guts. Victory here had been assured until the arrival of the damned Ultramarines, and Gurloch saw only too clearly that his own complacency had played its part in allowing them to upset his plans. He saw, also, that what his sorcerers said was true: tapping the powers of the warp could result in a swift and over-whelming victory here, but at the cost of all that he sought to achieve.

Gurloch had fought the Long War for ten thousand years, and he had not risen to lordship in that time by avoiding risk. He had faith, deep and festering. He knew that Nurgle would smile upon his endeavours. He had only to be courageous, and true to his purpose, and victory would be his.

Gurloch felt his skin crawl as though touched by a million twitching flies' wings. Thunder rumbled like the malevolent chuckle of a dark god, and emerald lightning danced through the clouds.

Cassian vaulted a toppled pillar and landed in the processional, barely a hundred yards from the fortress gates. He fired his bolt rifle from the hip, mowing down a gaggle of plague mutants, then drove his blade point first through the helm of a Plague Marine.

'With me!' he roared, his vox-amplified voice echoing over the battle. 'Ultramar! Ultramar!'

Cassian's battle-brothers surged around him, driving hard for the gates. The fortress loomed above them, a huge dark presence backlit by fierce green lightning. Its emplaced wall guns thundered, chewing lines of explosions through milling mutants and punching Plague Marines from their feet. Void shields thrummed, forming a protective dome that the loyalists now fought beneath.

The enemy still fought back, but it was a last gasp of defiance, nothing more. Plague Marines had dug themselves into the blasted ruins of hab-blocks lining the roadway, attempting to shoot at the Ultramarines while avoiding return fire from both in front and behind. It was not an enviable position, nor one that even the tenacious Death Guard could hold for long.

'Marcus,' voxed Cassian. 'It is time. Open the gates.'

'Understood, brother-lieutenant.'

A choral chime boomed out across the ruined city, and with a rumble of mighty engines the massive gates of the astropathic fortress began to swing open. As the gap between the slabs of adamantium widened, Cassian saw a sub-cloister beyond them, flanked by servitor guns and leading through to another set of gates beyond.

'Truly, the architects of this place meant for their charges to remain safe,' commented Dematris.

'Let us hope that – against all odds – they were successful,' said Cassian, gunning down another plague mutant.

The moment the gates were wide enough, Marcus' Reivers burst forth to join the fight. Now that stealth was no longer required, they entered battle as Guilliman intended, their skull masks vox-amplifying their war cries into terrifying roars and their bolt carbines blazing. They pelted a band of Plague Marines with stun grenades, sending the traitors reeling as their auto-senses were overloaded by modulating blasts of light, sound and spiritual chaff.

Cassian charged up the roadway, leading his brothers to link up with Marcus' warriors. Ahead of him, a twisted Death Guard alchemist emerged from amongst the ruins. The figure hurled a bloated projectile at Cassian, some kind of severed and stitched-up head. The lieutenant threw himself aside, and the projectile burst against the roadway where he had been. Slime sprayed, chewing deep holes in the ferrocrete.

Cassian rose smoothly into a firing crouch and put three bolt-rounds into the alchemist's helm from twenty yards. The Plague Marine convulsed as his head deformed then detonated, much like the disgusting weapons he had flung at Cassian and his battle-brothers. His carcass slumped, shattering the last of the alembics on his back and engulfing the Plague Marines in a cloud of such virulent foulness that even they could not withstand it.

'Victory!' Cassian roared. 'We have victory! Brothers, smash the last of them aside. Make for the gates!'

'Lieutenant,' said Keritraeus, and Cassian was pulled up short by the pain and alarm he heard. He glanced left to see the Librarian staggering and clutching his temples. His psychic hood was glowing brightly, wisps of smoke rising from its circuits.

'Something is coming,' said Keritraeus. The next instant, green lightning stabbed down from the heavens, a searing volley that struck again and again. All through the ruins, foul green smoke began to billow up from wherever the lightning struck.

'Move,' ordered Cassian. 'Get to sanctuary, now!'

But even as he gave the order, he saw that it was too late. The lightning speared down amidst Marcus' Reivers, throwing them aside and raising billowing fumes that filled the gateway. Amidst the churning fog banks, Cassian saw cadaverous figures moving; he heard the clang of rusted bells, the drone of bloated flies and the miserable chant of endless counting. Cyclopic yellow eyes stared out at him as the things trudged forwards to attack.

'Daemons,' said Keritraeus in grim resignation.

CHAPTER NINE

Daemons.

Anathema things, warp spawn formed from the unnatural energies of the empyrean and given sentience by the Dark Gods. They were the hellish get of the Emperor's ultimate foes, and for that, Dematris hated them more than all the traitors in the galaxy.

He hefted his crozius arcanum, checked the load on his absolvor bolt pistol and prepared to smite these unholy monsters in the Emperor's name.

'Dematris, Keritraeus,' shouted Cassian. 'We have to get inside the fortress. Shipmaster Aethor reports the main Death Guard force closing from the east. They'll be on us in moments. We can't let these abominations stop us when we're so close to victory.'

'Understood,' barked Dematris. 'I shall lead our brothers in a push on the gate.'

'We cannot risk committing our full force to this,'

said Cassian. 'We would be exposed to attack from the rear. I will retain a force of our brothers and block the road.'

'I will join you, lieutenant,' said Keritraeus. 'The foe wields fell sorcery – you will need my protection.'

'In the name of the primarch then,' said Dematris.

'And of the Emperor,' replied Cassian.

Dematris advanced up the processional towards the fortress gates. Plague-mutant corpses formed smouldering hillocks all around him, and unclean things were squirming out of the charnel heaps like maggots.

He could see what remained of Squad Marcus fighting furiously against the foul daemons that now surrounded them. The things were bloated monsters, their sloughing flesh pale and rotted, their faces ghastly masks of pus and buboes each boasting a single eye and a single horn. They clutched blades of rusted iron that they swung in ponderous arcs, while around them the air boiled with flies and plague spores.

'Aggressors, Inceptors, Brother Indomator – with me!' cried Dematris, his voice a vox-amplified roar. 'The enemy reveal themselves in all their foulness, yet these heretical filth-creatures are no match for the true defenders of humanity. Gather your hate! Gather your faith! These worthless things can withstand neither!'

Dematris launched himself into the fight. He swung his crozius into the back of a daemon's skull, and the thing's head exploded in a shower of slime. Even as its bubbling body dissolved into smoke, he was already firing his heavy-gauge bolt pistol, every round finding its mark in another rotting body. Explosions sprayed filth across his armour. Hellspawn staggered and groaned.

They were tough. For every one of the creatures he sent howling back to the warp, another would withstand his attacks, stumbling then rallying back to stab at him with its blade. Flies whirled around Dematris in a storm, blinding him as they tried frantically to find any chink in his armour.

'Foul spawn!' he roared. 'Filth incarnate! Unclean parodies! In the Emperor's name, I hurl you back into the abyss!'

Dematris kept swinging and firing, ignoring the rotted claws and rusted blades that raked across his power armour. He hewed a path to Sergeant Marcus' side.

'Tough bastards,' grunted Marcus, sawing his blade through a daemon's throat and kicking its dissolving body away from him. 'Fearless, too. Stun grenades do nothing.'

'Faith will do everything you need,' replied Dematris, and his tone brooked no argument. The mass of daemons pressed in from all sides, mumbling their endless, droning count as they fought. Thunder roared as the fortress' wall guns poured shots into the melee, bursting the daemons of Nurgle like sacks of wet offal. Reiver blades and bolt carbines felled more of the creatures.

Still they pressed in, and Dematris began to think he would be overwhelmed before the very gates he had vowed to secure.

Then came the blaring machine-voice of Brother Indomator, bellowing his war cry as he led the charge into the daemons' ranks. The Redemptor Dreadnought fired his macro plasma incinerator point-blank, and rotted horrors vanished in a flare of light. His massive power fist swept through them like a wrecking ball, hurling melting corpses high into the air. At Indomator's side fought the Aggressors of Squad Temeter, along with the bounding Inceptors of squads Polandrus and Thaddean.

Dematris shouted in triumph as the daemons were torn apart. Groaning voices turned thin and echoing, before fading altogether as the pack of daemons discorporated into sludge and smoke.

The Ultramarines were left panting with exertion, standing over the rusted and riven bodies of their dead. Yet the gate was theirs. Dematris opened a vox-channel to let the lieutenant know, but emerald lightning leapt again, and jaundiced smoke billowed up between Dematris' force and Cassian's. From within came the rumble and crackle of blazing furnaces, and the rusted creak of mechanical joints. Huge shapes moved amidst the murk.

'Back!' he cried. 'Secure the gates. Whatever comes, do not let it through, brothers. We cannot let the fortress fall.'

Gurgling roars shook the air, and from within the fume came tank-sized monsters, bloated things of leprous flesh and blazing eyes that trampled forwards on mechanical legs. The daemon engines flexed piston-driven claws and clutched foetid blades as tall as battle-brothers, and as they came they loosed a hail of shots from cannons sutured into their shoulder flesh.

'Hold!' roared Dematris as fire rained around him. 'Whatever the cost! Hold!'

* * *

Fifty yards down the processional, Cassian watched the Death Guard emerge from the ruins. The heretics' forces had been mauled, yet they still outnumbered his own warriors two to one at least. Foul champions led their advance: rot-cowled sorcerers and lumbering freaks that tolled monstrous bells or wielded filthy surgical instruments. Bloat-drones flew above them on smoke-belching turbines, their foul cannons pointed straight at the Ultramarines' lines.

Against this horde, he had his surviving Intercessors and Hellblasters dug in amongst the ruins, supported by the Dreadnought Brother Marius and the two battle-damaged Repulsors.

'There,' said Keritraeus. 'Their leader.'

Cassian followed the Librarian's gaze and saw a hulking warrior with a cracked, horned helm. With him marched several twisted Terminators.

'So much misery laid at that one's feet,' said Cassian. 'Whatever else happens here today, he will not walk away alive.'

'We need only hold them until Dematris secures the gate,' said Keritraeus.

'*If* Dematris secures the gate,' said Cassian, glancing doubtfully at the yellowed fog banks that lay thick across the processional.

With a glottal roar, the Death Guard began their attack. Hails of bolt shells tore into the ruins, blasting away rubble and striking sparks from blue power armour. Sprays of filth jetted into the Ultramarines' lines as the bloat-drones bombarded them.

'Fire!' roared Cassian.

Around him, his warriors let fly. The guns of the

Repulsor tanks screamed as they hosed shots into the advancing traitors. Brother Marius joined his fire to theirs, while the plasma incinerators of the Hellblasters spat glowing blasts that reduced heretics to ash.

The punishing firestorm intensified as the two battle-lines closed, and Cassian gripped the hilt of Duty tight. This was it – either the Death Guard would break them here, before the fortress walls, or they would hold out long enough to pull back through the gates and slam them in their enemies' faces.

It was to be a battle of attrition.

Cassian's eyes widened at the realisation. 'Don't give them the fight they desire. Keritraeus! Squad Gallen! On me! They are expecting us to dig in and try to outlast them, but you don't survive a disease simply by enduring. You cut out the canker at its source!'

'Their lord?' asked Keritraeus.

'Their lord,' echoed Cassian. 'Let us carve out the enemy's cancerous heart and see if they can survive without it.'

He surged from cover, bolt rifle roaring.

Gurloch saw his enemy coming. It was enough to return the smile to his rotten features.

'Ah! Some spirit after all!' he growled. 'Come to me, you hale lapdogs – let me dirty you with Nurgle's munificence.'

He revved the cutting teeth of his plaguereaper, and planted his feet in a fighting stance. Around him, the surviving Witherlings opened fire. The roar of their combi-bolters was deafening, and Gurloch chortled as he felt it shudder through his leprous bones.

One of the Ultramarines went down as a bolt-round punched through his faceplate. Another stumbled, then took a blight-shell straight to the chest. His body collapsed on itself in seconds, turning to blackened rot and rust.

The rest of the Space Marines dropped into firing crouches and let fly, their guns screaming with the distinctive fury of overcharge. Glowing bolts of energy slammed into the Witherlings: Gulgoth lost a leg at the knee and crashed over with a roar; Slurgh the Fatted took a shot to the gut, his armour dissolving and his straining belly bursting like an overripe blister; Nolghul Everlife was killed, his lifeless body toppling back like a felled statue.

One of the Ultramarines vanished in a plume of plasma and fire as his gun's machine-spirit rebelled, but it was small comfort to Gurloch.

At the same time, the two Space Marine leaders kept coming. A Librarian, and an officer or champion of a rank Gurloch didn't recognise.

'Come to me!' he bellowed. 'I am Gurloch of the Death Guard, and I will carve the names of my fallen into your rotting corpses!'

The loyalist champion came at him, firing his bolt rifle at Gurloch's face. The Lord of Contagion took the shots on his helm without flinching, then swung up his axe to block a swift blade stab. Power sword met plaguereaper in a shower of sparks, and the loyalist staggered back. Gurloch followed up, stomping forwards and swinging his weapon in a mighty arc that the Ultramarine only just dodged.

'Swarm him,' snarled Gurloch, and a droning mass

of flies whirled down upon the Ultramarine like a storm.

Blue lightning leapt, and Gurloch's flies fell from the air in fistfuls, crisped and dead. The rest dispersed with a frantic buzzing, revealing the Librarian with his staff still crackling.

Molghus, the last of the Witherlings, rushed the Librarian, firing as he went. His shots rebounded from a shield of force. The psyker's eyes blazed, and Molghus bellowed as white fire burst from the joints in his armour, blazing like plasma. Still he lunged at the Librarian, managing to slam his power mace into the psyker's chest-plate. The Librarian was thrown from his feet, before Molghus collapsed in a blackened heap.

Gurloch roared his anger – a terrible, bubbling sound.

'Unworthy!' he bellowed. 'You are unworthy of those you slay!'

He stormed towards the psyker, but staggered as another volley of bolt shots hit him in the side. The rounds blasted craters in his armour and sent splatters of flesh and slime across the ferrocrete. Gurloch turned angrily, just in time to catch the downswing of the Ultramarine officer's blade. It crackled blue as it struck his plaguereaper and mangled one of its buzz-saw blades.

In return, Gurloch stepped close, releasing his weapon's haft with one hand and grabbing the Space Marine's shoulder guard. His enemy tried to pull away as Gurloch's sweat-slick grasp rusted his armour, but he was nowhere near strong enough. With a deranged grin, Gurloch headbutted his enemy as hard as he could, crumpling the Ultramarine's faceplate and shattering the lenses of his helm.

Gurloch raised his axe to grind its whirring teeth into the loyalist's face, only for a blast of psychic energy to hit him from behind. Gurloch staggered, dropping the dazed Ultramarine, and turned with a furious growl to face the Librarian again.

'Enough!' he roared, and lumbered towards his tormentor. Plasma blasts screamed around him, one striking his armour with enough force to sear a blackened crater in his ribs. The Librarian hurled lightning at Gurloch, causing agony to race through the Chaos lord's body and his armour to smoulder, but still Gurloch forged on, Nurgle's gifts pouring fresh vitality through his flesh even as it blackened and died.

He raised his plaguereaper high, then swung it down with killing force.

Cassian's head cleared, and he hissed in pain as he tore his mangled helm free. His nose was shattered. One eye was blinded, and he winced as he pulled a shard of lens-glass from his bloody socket. The tainted rain dribbled into his wounds, making them burn and ache.

Yet his pain was forgotten in an instant as he saw Gurloch bearing down on Keritraeus.

'No!' he shouted, reaching for his blade, stumbling to his feet, knowing he was too late.

The axe fell.

Keritraeus' staff sheared in two as he tried to block the blow. Churning blades swept through the Librarian's gorget, then his neck, then out the back of his armour in a spray of blood and sparks. His head thumped to the ferrocrete, still attached to a mangled mass of flesh, bone and armour. His corpse fell next to it, bright Adeptus Astartes blood flooding into the oily puddles.

Around Cassian, his battle-brothers were fighting as best they could, holding the enemy back despite the odds. One of their tanks was now a blazing wreck, and Brother Marius was limping on a ruined leg. The enemy pressed in from all sides.

He had led them to this.

He would not betray them by giving in now.

'Dematris,' he shouted over the vox. 'Either the gate is secure or we are all dead men. One way or another, I'm ordering all battle-brothers to fall back on your position now!'

With his order given, Cassian shook the rain from his blade, spat a wad of blood and charged Lord Gurloch.

The hulking brute saw him coming and leered through a rent in his helm. He was bloated, enormous, reeking of power and filth. Yet he was wounded sorely; Cassian's comrades had seen to that.

'Emperor,' bellowed Cassian, 'lend strength to my arm!'

He came in hard, swinging his sword in a beheading arc. His enemy parried, far faster than his corpulent frame would suggest was possible, and their weapons clanged together again.

'Your Emperor has no strength to give,' laughed Gurloch. 'He is weak. Impotent. Just like you.'

The two warriors swung and parried amidst the driving rain. Thunder boomed overhead, the Dark Gods themselves urging the Death Guard on to victory.

In his peripheral vision, Cassian saw his surviving men falling back in good order, blitzing fire into the Death Guard as they followed his orders and left him behind. That was good, he thought. Victory demanded sacrifice.

There was another clashing exchange of blades, and Cassian was driven back again, with a bloody rent in his chest and another in his thigh. He had wounded his enemy again and again, but the Chaos lord didn't seem to feel it.

'Give up, lapdog,' said Gurloch, his tone almost kindly. 'With every heartbeat, the gifts of Grandfather Nurgle crawl through your bloodstream and bring you closer to death, even as they fortify my magnificent form with fresh might. I have opened myself to his generosity, but for you, I fear, the burden of his boons may prove too much. This is a fight you cannot win.'

Cassian shook his head, feeling the truth of his enemy's words. His body burned with fever heat and shuddered with sudden chills. His vision swam. A momentary glance at his wounds confirmed that they were festering and blackening by the moment.

'Strike swift,' he gasped to himself. 'Strike true. Cut out… the canker.'

Marshalling the last of his strength, Cassian hurled his bolt rifle at Gurloch's head. Surprised, the Chaos lord swatted the weapon away with the blade of his axe. In that moment, Cassian hurled himself at his enemy, swinging his sword down in a thunderous overarm blow that left him wide open to attack.

Gurloch brought his plaguereaper back around. Its churning blades slammed into Cassian's midriff and bit deep. Yet even the Chaos lord's prodigious might was not enough to stop Duty slamming down onto the crest of his helm. Ceramite and diseased flesh split open like an infected wound as the power sword carved down through Gurloch's skull and into the diseased meat of his brain.

Cassian stumbled back, rent armour sparking, blood pouring from the massive wound in his stomach. He felt his legs going cold. Dimly, he saw the hilt of his power sword jutting out from just above Gurloch's jaw. It had split the Chaos lord's head clean in two.

Gurloch's mouth worked, a drizzle of rancid gore and wriggling maggots spilling from it. He pawed one-handedly at the hilt of the blade that had killed him. Then, at last, even the gifts of his foul god could no longer keep him on his feet.

Lord Gurloch fell, crashing to the wet stone, and Cassian followed him down. Over the vox, he half heard the bellows of Chaplain Dematris. He deciphered the words *gates secure* and something about *falling back within*.

It was enough. Knowing that he had done all that he could for his primarch, Lieutenant Cassian let the darkness take him.

EPILOGUE

Cassian lay beneath a pall of shadows. There was no sound, no sensation. No pain. His sense of self drifted, and for a time he felt nothing but a strange kind of peace.

Something moved. A figure, tall and powerful. Cassian saw for a moment the grotesque mass of the Death Guard lord, and he felt a shudder of panic grip him. Yet the hand that drew back his shroud was gentle, and the face that looked down upon him was regal and beatific. A halo of light shimmered around it, and in his mind Cassian heard the distant voices of angelic choirs swell.

'Lieutenant Cassian,' said the figure, and his voice was as firm and reassuring as bedrock.

'Em... per... or?' asked Cassian, his voice little more than a croak.

The figure smiled.

'Once, almost, for my sins. Lieutenant, is your duty done?'

Part of Cassian wanted to nod, to say yes, that he had given everything: his men, his comrades. His life.

Instead, he shook his head in a single, jerky motion. 'Only in… death… does duty… end…'

The figure's smile vanished, replaced by something sterner, tinged with sorrow and pride. Cassian hoped never to forget the power of that gaze.

'Very well, lieutenant,' said the figure. Slowly, he replaced the shroud over Cassian's face, and as he did so, darkness closed in once more.

Cassian woke, and for a moment believed that he was truly dead. He hung in darkness, and could feel nothing at all.

Then he heard a voice, filtering to him as though through a vox.

'Vitals online. Synaptic choristry aligning. Bio-auguries look good, all runes in the green. Full sensorium coming online… now.'

Cassian tried to blink as light flooded his vision, yet even his eyelids seemed numbed. The pain swiftly subsided as he adjusted to the sudden restoration of his sight, and he realised that he was in a shipboard apothecarion. Three Apothecaries whom he didn't recognise crowded around him. To his surprise, there was a Techmarine with them.

Suddenly, data-feeds began scrolling down his peripheral vision. He could see power levels, reactor-stability readings, vox and auspex data. Realisation began to dawn as he tried to look down at himself, only to feel a jarring sense of dislocation.

'I… cannot feel my body,' he said, and his voice was a vox-generated rumble.

'It is alright, brother,' said one of the Apothecaries. 'Your body was ravaged beyond our abilities to restore. We saved only those parts you would need.'

'I… would need…?' Cassian knew what they were saying, but even as the conditioned part of his psyche processed the revelation, another part of his mind was screaming in panic and trying desperately to move limbs that weren't there, flex muscles that didn't exist and feel skin that he no longer possessed.

'You made a great sacrifice, brother,' said a familiar voice, and the others parted to reveal Fourth Company Captain Adrastean, clad in his shipboard robes and smiling a tight smile. 'You gave up your body of flesh in the name of victory. These fine brothers have given you another, that you might continue to fight.'

'I am… a Dreadnought,' said Cassian, feeling a chill as the realisation sank in. He was organs, now. Biological component parts: a brain, hearts, lungs, veins, arteries and vulnerable innards – bound within an amniotic weave and entombed within the armoured sarcophagus of a Redemptor.

Part of him felt pride, and a thankfulness that he was not dead. The other part tried to vocalise its claustrophobic horror, but with an effort, he strangled that voice into silence. Some warriors went mad upon internment within a Dreadnought body. He would not shame himself by joining their number.

'You are a Dreadnought,' said Adrastean.

'How? My men? Were we victorious?'

'Thanks in no small part to the heroic sacrifices made by yourself and Brother-Librarian Keritraeus, you were,' replied Adrastean. 'As I understand it, when you slew the enemy leader it caused no small degree of havoc amongst the Death Guard. Many of their high-ranking lieutenants must already have been dead. Their command structure was in tatters. In the confusion, Chaplain Dematris was able not only to pull the strike force back within the safety of the walls, but to lead a swift offensive that drove the foe from your vicinity and allowed for recovery of both your and Keritraeus' bodies.'

Cassian took a moment to process this, feeling his senses gradually synching with those of his unfamiliar metal body. He realised that he could look through multiple optic actuators at once. As he did so, he noticed that his new body was, for the moment, limbless and suspended in an intricate web of wires and armatures.

'How did we get here?' he asked. 'Where *is* here? Did we make it back to the Indomitus Crusade fleet?'

'In fact,' said Adrastean, 'the crusade fleet made it to you. We received your astropathic message and sent a substantial force to effect your safe extraction.'

'There was a plague. Within the walls. Everyone was dead.'

'Not the astropathic choir. When the Death Guard first attacked, the choirmaster withdrew them within a psy-baffled refuge chamber. They and a few senior members of the fortress' personnel quarantined themselves inside. Dematris found them, exhausted and close to starvation, within the fortress' inner sanctum. He had them send a message, and keep sending it until half their number had died from warp trauma or physical exhaustion. But against the odds, they broke through the storms and made contact. Our ships arrived above Kalides five days later.'

'Five days?' asked Cassian. 'The strike force held out that long?'

'They did,' said Adrastean proudly. 'With Dematris' leadership and the fortress walls to shield them, they dug in and resisted the Death Guard's every effort to break through. Without their leader to drive them onwards, and with whatever ritual they intended in tatters, the enemy seemed to lose heart. Of course, the *Primarch's Sword* punished them with heavy bombardments whenever its auspex were able to divine their locations. And once we had multiple ships in orbit, and fresh waves of Space Marines deploying to the surface...'

'The Death Guard were defeated,' finished Cassian with relish.

'They were annihilated.'

'What of Kalides Prime?'

'Declared purgatus extremis. There was little enough to save. We bombed the astropathic fortress into rubble, destroyed any remaining viable military assets and laced the lower atmosphere with enough servitor-mines to ensure that, should the Death Guard return for their warriors, they will receive a deeply unpleasant welcome.'

Cassian was quiet for a moment, feeling the tick and whirr of systems within his strange new body.

'Captain,' he said eventually, 'I wish to serve penance.'

'Penance?' asked Adrastean.

'I lost over half of the warriors under my charge. I let Keritraeus die, and was very nearly slain myself. I cost the lives of every Cadian on Kalides, and barely succeeded in extracting any of my strike force at all. I failed in my duty, and deserve penance.'

Before Adrastean could reply, the doors to the apothecarion whispered open and a towering figure ducked through. Cassian's hearts thumped faster as he recognised the magnificent figure of the primarch – Roboute Guilliman, here in person.

Around Cassian, the other Ultramarines dropped to one knee. He felt his shame and frustration grow as he instinctively tried – and failed – to do the same.

'Brother Cassian,' said Guilliman, fixing him with an unreadable expression.

'My lord,' said Cassian, 'I am not worthy to be in your presence.'

'You are not just worthy, my son – you are a hero. I will hear no more talk of failure.'

'I…' Cassian was lost for words.

'You were thrown wildly off course by catastrophic warp storms,' continued Guilliman. 'Having already completed the mission that I sent you to accomplish, you not only held your force together through that dire experience, but you then successfully identified a means by which you could get word to us of your plight. You engaged a force of Heretic Astartes several times the size of your own, whose plan would, I suspect, have caused devastation and misery across multiple systems. I am reliably informed that you showed nothing short of an absolute dedication to the completion of your mission, shrugged off a crushing defeat and alien interference, and even gave your own life to ensure the downfall of the foe. To me, Brother Cassian, those are the actions not of a failure, but of a hero.'

Cassian's mind reeled, and fierce pride burned within him as he felt the sincerity of his primarch's words.

'Thank you, my lord,' he managed, as around him the other Ultramarines officers stood and offered him a warrior's salute.

'You will be properly honoured for your valour,' said Guilliman. 'The commensurate accolades will be graven upon your sarcophagus by the artificers before we next go into battle.'

Cassian tried to nod, and realised he couldn't. 'Thank you, my lord.'

'Thank me by learning to wield that mighty new body of yours in battle, Cassian,' said the primarch with a smile. 'We are only three days out from the Tarchoria Front. Do you think you will be battle-ready in that time?'

'Give me my limbs, my weapons,' said Cassian fiercely, 'and I will train every moment until we make planetfall, my lord.'

'Good,' said Guilliman, smile broadening. 'Are you ready to keep fighting, Dreadnought-Brother Cassian?'

'I am, my lord,' said Cassian, feeling a surge of purpose like a flame within him. 'The crusade must continue!'

'And so it shall, until the last heretic lies dead and my father's realm is restored at last to glory.'

'For Ultramar!' cried the Space Marines, and Cassian shouted with them.

'For humanity,' said Guilliman. 'Before it is too late.'